SWEET
DIAMOND DUST

Cover design by Asher Kingsley and Barbara Leff
Book design by Iris Bass
Author photograph by Joel Bregar

SWEET
DIAMOND DUST

by
ROSARIO FERRÉ

Translated from the Spanish by the Author

BALLANTINE BOOKS • NEW YORK

An Available Press Book
Published by Ballantine Books

Translation copyright © 1988 by Rosario Ferré

All rights reserved under International and Pan-American Copyright
Conventions. Published in the United States of America by Ballantine
Books, a division of Random House, Inc., New York, and simultaneously
in Canada by Random House of Canada Limited, Toronto. Originally
published in Spanish as *Maldito Amor* by Editorial Joaquin Mortiz,
S.A. de C.V., Mexico in 1986. Copyright © 1986 by Editorial Joaquin
Mortiz, S.A. de C.V.

Library of Congress Catalog Card Number: 88-92156
ISBN 0-345-34778-1

Manufactured in the United States of America

First American Edition: January 1989

To my parents, and to their parents before them.

To Gautier Benítez and to Juan Morel Campos.

CONTENTS

Es hielo abrasador, es fuego helado,
es herida que duele y no se siente,
es un soñado bien, un mal presente
es un breve descanso muy cansado.

FRANCISCO DE QUEVEDO

Perla que el mar de entre su concha arranca
al agitar sus ondas placenteras,
garza dormida entre la espuma blanca
del níveo cinturón de tus riberas.

JOSÉ GAUTIER BENÍTEZ

I.

SWEET DIAMOND DUST

I.

GUAMANÍ

"IN THE PAST THE PEOPLE OF GUAMANÍ USED TO BE PROUD of their town and of their valley. From the red-ochered cliffs that pour their blood upon the valley every day at three o'clock, when the inevitable afternoon showers burst upon it, we loved to behold our town nestled on the silvery arms of Ensenada Honda bay. Having finished the day's chores, we liked to drive up to Hawk Nest's Point and sit there awhile, admiring its sparkling clean streets, its houses spreading their balconied verandahs upon the slopes like a debutante's brightly colored skirts, its bright-yellow cathedral, with the shimmering plume of its belfry and the red-tiled crest of its dome, preening like a bird of paradise in their midst, and the townspeople running frantically to and fro, as they took cover from the pelting, gaily pealing rain that fell from the scudding dove-breasted clouds.

At that time, many years ago, we were convinced Guamaní was the most beautiful town on the island. Built on the gently rolling slopes that descend from Mount Guamaní, it

3

looks upon a savannah of fabulously fertile loam, whose sabled, furrowed topsoil is considered to be one of the richest in the world. Our town had lived, up to the turn of the century, from the produce of this soil, which the residents revered and took meticulous care of, as the most precious gift their forebears, the Taino aborigines, had bequeathed them. In Taino legends, all living things on the island—men, animals, and plants alike—had been born from the sacred caves of Cacibajagua in Mount Guamaní, dwelling place of the god Yuquiyú. It was because the residents of Guamaní considered themselves to be the children of their mountain, which resembled from afar a huge green velvet breast, that they were a peaceful people, leery of war and ready to share what little they owned with their neighbors. In ancient times they had revered the mountain that towered above them, and under Spanish rule every Guamaneño had, hidden away in his home, a polished stone idol carved in its image and likeness. The stone's Taino name was Cemí, but as the Spaniards punished its worshipers with death, the Guamaneño's called them lightning stones, and when they were found in their homes by the suspicious Guardia Civil or by church officials, they swore they didn't know where they came from but that they fell on their heads from heaven every time it rained. As time went by, the Guamaneños themselves forgot that the name of the strange stones was Cemí, or that they were household deities that their forebears held in homage as benefactors of the home, but they never threw them out, and they kept them hidden and half-forgotten under gaily colored shawls at the bottom of their sandalwood chests, or glimmering like strange, ink-dark diamonds behind jars of coriander and basil, ájilimójili and alioli, sweet chili peppers, cloves, and garlics, concealed high on the farthest shelves of their cupboards.

Guamaní's main crop has always been sugarcane, and the townspeople lived from the bustling commerce produced around half a dozen small sugar mills that had sprung up around it during the nineteenth century. But cane sugar was not the only dry staple they traded in. From our orchards and vegetable patches at the time there grew, as in the candid paradises that Le Douanier Rousseau painted in his canvases, a leafy, exuberant profusion of fruits and vegetables that adorned our tables and embellished our dinners with the arabesques of their delicately steamed perfumes. In them grew the claret-red yautia as well as the paled, sherried golden one, the velvety kind that grew in Vieques and the bristly, bearded one, which resembled a conquistador's pugnacious jaw and whose glories of the palate were sung by Gonzalo Fernández de Oviedo in his *Natural History of the Indies*, and prepared by Guamaneños in their world-famous fritters, which sizzled in their mouths in boisterous bursts of epicurean laughter; the tumultuous tom tom taro roots, brought by African slaves on the wailing ships of death, which they named Ñáñigo and Farafanga, Mussumba and Tomboctú, in honor of their towering raven kings, always decked out in battle finery, and which we innocently reaped from our gardens as one digs out a snow-filled mammoth's foot; the wintry white cassava and the one that flamed unseen beneath the earth, sparking under our feet to the rhythms of Yucuba and Tubaga, Diacana and Nubaga, Congolese deities of long-lost faraway forests, which Guamaneños used to knead into the perfumed loaves that blessed their homes; the poisonous, treacherous cassava streaked with purple orchid's veins, which the Tainos and the African slaves used to drink when they were about to be tortured by the Spaniards, and which we now keep hidden in cobalt jars at the back of our mahogany wardrobes as a pious last resource; the honeyed yam and the thick-lipped one that leaves you moonstruck if you eat it at night; the mysteriously aphrodisiac gingerroot, with emerald swords unsheathed and blooming lips pursed in blood, which afforded us a profitable smuggling trade all through the nineteenth century; the golden ripe plantain and the green one with silver tips, quivering on the branches of Mafafo and Malango trees, undisputed monarchs of the Guamaneño's table and forefathers of the saintly pionono as well as of the infidel mofongo, the tostón, and the empanada; the exotic alcapurria, that savory Muslim queen, wrapped in its golden Moorish veils that melted on the tongue; the paradise pineapple and the sugar loaf, the one brought from Yayama and the

one brought from Yayagua, which the Spaniards named *piña*
out of vengeance pure and simple, because they never had
anything like it at home, though it resembled the pine nut as
much as the duck a swan; the Persian avocado and the
Malayan breadfruit; the ripe guava pear singing high up on
the branch, 'a jealous man never sleeps, but spies on his
beautiful wife.' And presiding over all of this the fragrant
suckling pig, slowly turning on its perfumed branch over the
smoking embers; a golden deity sacrificed to an even greater
glory of the senses, a crackling, sizzling, barbarous delight of
which the ears, the snout, the curlicued tail, the labyrinthine
blood sausages spiced with Hottentot peppercorns were the
horror of our foreign visitors and the most exquisite morsel of
our holy day feasts.

   And it wasn't just the lushness of our valley that made us
feel proud and content. Well-to-do families lived in elegant
houses, with wood-carved lace fans filtering the afternoon
rays of the sun over their doorways, balconies of marble
balusters to let in the breeze, and polished domino floors. At
that time Guamaneños of the upper crust all belonged to the
same clan. There were blood ties among the most distant
families, and we always gave one another financial and moral
support, so as better to manage our sugarcane haciendas. Our
sons studied in Europe and our daughters were taught the
sacred virtues of the home. Our social and cultural activities
were always in the best of tastes: the men never went to
church, rode their spirited polo ponies, and practiced rifle-
shooting every afternoon, and in the evenings would pay a
visit to Guamaní's casino, where they played dominos, rou-
lette, and baccarat; the women went to mass every day and
visited one another at home, where they played rummy, fan
fan, and checkers; and did constant charity work at the
orphanage, as well as at the homes for the aged and for the
blind. Vulgarity and mediocrity were banished from our
midst, and we were faithfully present at the recitals of Adelina
Patti, the famous Italian opera singer, as well as at those of
the famed actress Eleonora Duse and the dancer Ana Pavlova,
who periodically visited Guamaní's Atheneum. We played
only classical music in banquets and balls, and our daughters

floated gracefully like gauze gardenias on the waves of the 'Blue Danube,' as they were whirled by their partners under the starry skies of our tropical nights. It was, no doubt about it, an innocent, guiltless world, and it is thus that our great Gautier Benítez immortalized it in his poems, it was thus that our great Morel Campos sang of it in his *danzas*. A world of austere pleasures and strenuous endeavors, of pleasure boating on the silvered surface of Ensenada Honda, picnics on the blue slopes of Mount Guamaní, and melancholy *danzas* waltzed under the wistful shadows of a whispering pine tree. A happy world no doubt, although poor and backward, in which one could forswear, as an unforgivable insult to one's dignity, everything that wasn't noble, exceptional, or beautiful.

Today all that has changed. Far from being a paradise, Guamaní has become a hell, a monstrous whirlpool from which the terrifying funnel of Snow White Sugar Mills spews out sugar night and day toward the north."

II.

THE MARRIAGE OF DOÑA ELVIRA

"The marriage between Doña Elvira De la Valle (also known in Guamaní as Doña Elvira of the four Ds: Del Roble, De la Cerda, De la Valle, and De Juan Ponce de León) and Don Julio Font took place soon after Doña Elvira's return from her studies in Europe. An only child, she had lost her mother and father at an early age, and her maiden aunts, Doña Emilia and Doña Estefana, had brought her up. Somehow they had managed to find enough money to send her to study in Paris, where she had acquired very refined tastes. Doña Elvira met Don Julio, a well-reputed Spaniard who lived by importing dry goods such as rice, sausage, codfish, and beans of all sizes and colors, into the country, in a *paso fino* exhibition in Guamaní. The town was famous for its horse shows or *'bellas formas,'* tournaments where our native Guamaneños excelled in expert demonstrations, such as riding their spirited steeds with such refined control that they could carry crystal water goblets filled to the brim in their hands without spilling a drop, or training their stallions al-

ways to bow before the ladies, complying thus with the rules
of etiquette of our casino and other elegant social clubs. The
judges had just granted first prize to Don Julio's mare, when
it halted before the gaily colored tarpaulin of the spectators'
platform and refused to walk on. Don Julio, who had been
observing Doña Elvira for a while as she sat in the shadowed
galleries, alighted unhurriedly from his mare and withdrew
the blue silk bow the judges had just pinned on its front
harness. He then walked, bow in hand, toward Doña Elvira,
and said out loud so that everyone could hear him: 'We all
know who the real winner is today, ladies and gentlemen, so
don't let's kid ourselves. Piel Canela also acknowledges it,
and that's why she won't walk on.' And, handing Doña
Elvira the blue silk bow, he begged her to keep it safe for him
until they should meet again.

Doña Elvira stared at him in wonderment. Don Julio's
brazen assault, totally lacking in the cloying embellishments
of Guamaneñan society, pleased her strangely, and she was
immediately conquered by it. Don Julio had been born in
the inhospitable cattle prairies of Lérida. His manner, so
different from the filigreed bowing and scraping of her previ-
ous wooers, seemed to her very attractive. So, laughing at
Don Julio's joke with her girl friends, Doña Elvira blush-
ingly accepted his gift and returned home as in a dream.

Enraptured in her fantasy world, she roamed the corridors
and sitting rooms of her aunts' house, daydreaming of Don
Julio's amber-colored eyes and returning to reality only when
she sat down at the piano to sing her favorite *danzas*. She
loved to play above all Juan Morel Campos's 'Maldito Amor,'
and after she met Don Julio she used to sing it at least ten
times a day, enjoying the sound of its lamenting arpeggios as
they spilled over the house's tall garden wall:

> Your love is now a songless bird
> Your love, my dear, is lost in my heart
> I don't know why your passion wilts me
> And why it never flamed!

Worried by their niece's anemic state, Doña Emilia and
Doña Elvira decided to invite Don Julio to come pay them a

visit at the house. Vigorous defenders of conjugal love and its advantages, they abetted the love affair from the start, and no more than two months went by before a date was set for the wedding. Don Julio, in addition to being handsome, was a hard-working man, and he could some day become an able administrator of Diamond Dust Sugar Mills. Both old ladies were totally dependent on the income they received from the mill for their survival, and they worried about the fact that the business had already been struggling for many years, without a man of the family at its head.

Don Julio took his job of administrator of Diamond Dust seriously. Once the wedding was over, he insisted on leaving the comfortable house the aunts had in the town, and decided to settle with Doña Elvira in the country.

'If you own a business, you must either tend it or sell it, unless you don't mind someone else pinching your profits,' he told his wife with a good-natured laugh, when she complained to him about the decision he had made. He'd never be one of those laced and stockinged gentlemen farmers, who loved to live it up in town while their overseers swindled them back at the hacienda, and he wanted to supervise personally the cutting of the sugar drops and the beginning of the grinding season.

Elvira said good-bye to her aunts and abided by her husband's wishes without further complaints. Once they had moved to the house in the country, she threw herself body and soul into her heavy chores. She was a small woman with a delicate frame, but she had a passionate soul. Once she had made certain they were there to stay, she told her husband:

'I've pleased you in everything; now it's your turn to make me happy. I want to make some improvements to the house, so I won't feel that we're living like louts, at the buttocks of the world.'

Elvira had good reason for her demands. The house was very old, and lacked even the most elementary sanitary facilities. There was no flush toilet and no running water, and one had to move one's bowels on a curious aerial latrine, perched at the end of a balustered balcony that jutted out over the windy canefields. It was surrounded by a screen of blue louvered windows that assured its privacy, and that had been built for the De la Valle family by a French architect more than a hundred years before.

'I can't understand why you keep complaining so,' Don Julio told her jokingly, as they looked the sandalwood latrine over together, admiring its mother-of-pearl lid. 'After all, it's an aristocratic antique, and finding relief over the canefields, abandoning one's ass to the perfumed tropical breezes while one fertilizes the harvest, can be an enchanting experience.'

Doña Elvira pressed her lips together and went back to her household chores, steeped in a bitter silence. A few days later she mentioned the fact once more to Don Julio, while she sat fanning herself on the balcony, on the rocking chair next to his. She must absolutely have a bidet and a washbasin, she said, as well as a bathtub where she could take a proper bath every day. She was ashamed to invite her friends to come and visit her, when she didn't even have a white porcelain tub, with the griffon claws, moon-sized silver shower head, and cabriole legs that were now so much in fashion. Don Julio, however, paid even less attention to her entreaties.

'We live like kings in this place, but you take everything for granted,' he answered her disagreeably. 'This island is a paradise, and you're not even aware of it. In Spain one must do without such comforts, and we never complain about it. In winter the cold makes your bones turn to ice shards, and in summer water must be hauled for twenty miles away in mule packs. The conquistadors were born in my province, and this is why they could conquer Mexico and Peru with only a handful of men. It was the land that made them into heros. It tempered them with sacrifice and deprivation, which are always commendable for the soul. That's why this island's elegant gentry are such good-for-nothing rakes, because they've become softened by luxury and indolence, warmed by tropical breezes, and used to living without needing to work. Like your conceited and dissolute friends in town, for example, whose greatest ambition is to become world authorities in art, music, and literature, while they let the lands they have inherited from their ancestors go fallow and fall to pieces.' As a consequence of Don Julio's speech,

Doña Elvira had to go on cooking in her coal stove, lighting her way down the dark corridors of the house with oil lamps, and carrying the water from the nearby spring in large metal lard cans every time she wanted to take a bath.

One day Don Julio decided it was imperative to increase the sugar production of the mill, and gave orders so that on every untilled plot of ground, on every vegetable and garden orchard hoed by the peons who harvested in their free time their own crops, a new sugar bed should be seeded. It had been the custom of the old masters of Diamond Dust to leave those fields that were most distant from the mill, at the edge of the hacienda itself, in the care of the day laborers, so that they could let their meager herds of goat and cattle graze in the lank, salty marshes of the hinterlands. Here they would also plant their exotic viands and victuals, such as the golden yam and the snowy taro root, which they would slowly stew in their traditional *sancouches*. The De la Valles were used to fealty and took for granted the loyalty of their tenants; in fact, thanks to this situation they had always lived like counts. But they had also maintained, through their sense of fidelity and retribution, a delicate balance between vassal and lord. For this reason, their servants and laborers worshiped them and had remained faithful even through the worst of crises. The De la Valles, for example, were godfathers to all their dependents' children and would always be present at their christenings, weddings, and wakes, which they attended dressed in all their finery and surrounded by an aura of stateliness, during which they traditionally bestowed their largesse, handing out large bags of coins and brightly wrapped gifts.

On the day that Doña Elvira learned Don Julio had decreed that the peasants' communal lands were to be taken from them in order to be seeded with sugarcane, she went looking for her husband in the cellar, where he kept the Humboldt deposit box he had had specially built in Germany. She had to knock several times before he heard her. The concrete walls of the safe were four feet deep, and the door was made of solid steel.

'The De la Valles have always been gentlemen farmers,

never slave traders,' she said when he finally opened the door. 'Your miserliness will bring calamity upon us, and you'll end up by drowning Diamond Dust in an ocean of sugarcane.'

Don Julio looked at her through the open door of the safe, surrounded by the cool vapors breathed forth by the bags of gold stacked in orderly rows behind him. He was surprised at her vehemence: he had given strict orders that no one should disturb him when he locked himself in the cellar. He told himself he had to be patient; *paso fino* mares were wont to be willful and gnash at the bit of the most experienced horseman. He waited a few seconds before answering his wife. 'It's not my fault if it rains every day at three o'clock in the afternoon in your piss-pot town, Elvirita,' he said with a smile. 'The recent rains have caused me a lot of damage, and God won't pay me back the interest rates.'

Doña Elvira realized that her husband was a skinflint with an iron elbow, and she went silently back to the kitchen, but a few days later she faced him again determinedly on another matter. Don Calixto Díaz, an old Negro workman who had been her father's slave, had caught his right arm in the iron presses of the mill, and the laborers had run once more to her rooms, clamoring for help. With her skirts rolled up to her knees, Doña Elvira had dashed across the muddy expanse that separated the machine sheds from the rambling old house and entered the mill. When she arrived at Don Calixto's side, the blood oozed out slowly from his elbow, making the dark-green syrup of the crushed canes turn bright red as it boiled at the bottom of the cauldron. Not for a second did she lose her self-control. She ordered that the presses be carefully turned in the opposite direction, and she herself helped to extract the man's crushed limb from its iron stranglehold.

That night, once she had finished praying her rosary beads next to her husband, and having covered herself with the heavy linen sheets of the De la Valles' marriage bed, she said to Don Julio: 'If you can't give that man back his arm, at least have a pension paid out to him for the rest of his days.' And she added that the accident had been his fault, because he had put Don Calixto, who was old and half-blind, in charge of the supervision of the mill's presses. There was a deep silence in the room, broken only by the bed's lacy canopy, which rustled faintly above the couple's heads as though swaying them peacefully to sleep. Don Julio had been spinning the thin thread of patience for months, and at that moment it finally broke. He sat up slowly in bed and lighted the gas lamp that stood on the night table next to him.

'If tomorrow you insisted that the Virgin Mary's last name was also De la Valle, I shouldn't be surprised,' he told her, trembling with rage, as he landed the first blow. 'From today onward, in this house women may speak when chickens start to pee, and I forbid you to go on meddling in other people's business.' And as he struck her left and right, he added that her saintly De la Valles, like the rest of Guamaní's hacienda owners of yore, had also been slave drivers, and that she was mad if she truly believed that it had been by casting out gold doubloons to the Negroes that well brought up girls were sent to study in Paris, could shit in imperial latrines, and took perfumed baths in authentic marble tubs, resting on griffon legs and decorated with gilded wings, won at the Victory of Samothrace.

Spent by Don Julio's ill treatment, Doña Elvira eventually ceased to take interest in the hacienda's blustering activities. She forsook her domestic chores and sank into a foggy silence, coming out of her mute despair only from time to time, when she would sit down at the piano to sing 'Maldito Amor,' her favorite *danza*. Don Julio, for his part, became more and more absorbed by the tasks of the sugar mill. He soon tired of eating his meals in silence, facing a sullen woman with dark eyes rimmed in purple, and began to invite his brutish friends, the mill's overseer and foreman, to share them with him. Their coarse jokes and bellowing laughter echoed through the house at all hours of the night, as they enjoyed together the bottles of moonshine rum that they themselves illegally distilled.

Doña Elvira had just given birth to Ubaldino De la Valle, Guamaní's most eminent statesman, and was fulfilling in bed the traditional forty days of San Gerardo's postpartum convalescence, when Diamond Dust was leveled by one of the most fearful hurricanes of the century. The sky had split open in a cataclysm of wind, which had whirled away the ironwood gabled ceiling of the house as though it were a paper hat, and a deluge of water had suddenly poured over them. The family took refuge in the foul depths of the cellar, where the mosquitoes had bred by thousands in the putrid air, as they waited for the wind's fury to abate. They were forced to stay there for almost a month, while Diamond Dust blazed on all sides like a subsidiary of hell, since Don Julio never found time to haul back the ceiling of their house, which had landed twenty miles away, in a neighbor's cattle trough. He was too busy supervising the kindling of the sugar crops before they began to rot, buried as they were under an avalanche of mud. Lying ill on her iron cot and forced to drink from the waters of the nearby spring, which had also become turbulent and turbid with mud, Doña Elvira became infected with typhoid fever and died soon after. As she lay dying she pitifully cried out for a priest, but was deprived of the comforts of our Holy Church's last rites. It was thus that Ubaldino De la Valle, our gallant political leader and patriot, was born; and it was thus that he found himself abandoned, when he was a few days old, in the arms of his wet nurse, Doña Encarnación Rivera, who suckled him and took care of him until he came of age."

III.

THE CONSULTATION

YES, IT'S BEEN FIVE YEARS SINCE NIÑO UBALDINO PROMISED us the cottage we've always lived in, since we began working for him thirty years ago, and that's why we've come to see you today, Don Hermenegildo. The house is a nice piece of property. It sits at the back of the garden of the big house, so that we only have to walk a few steps to reach the master's kitchen and laundry room; it has a sturdy zinc roof and a covered balustered balcony where we can dry our clothes out when it rains. You were always a good friend of his and would visit often at the house. I remember serving you a cup of freshly brewed coffee with a shot of rum in it more than once, and you were always very kind and courteous toward me. It was Néstor who by chance saw the sign on the door as he went by your office a few days ago, when he came to town to buy groceries: Don Hermenegildo Martínez, Notary Lawyer. He must have seen it a hundred times before but it never occurred to him who it was until he saw the second sign, which recently went up next to the first one: President

16

of the Paso Fino Association. He realized then it must be you, the Don Hermenegildo who used to sit talking with Niño Ubaldino for hours on end about the equestrian arts, the filigreed exploits of dancing mares at the last exhibition, or the rising costs of purebred studs on the island, and he made up his mind to see you. Only he's shy, and at the last moment he made me come instead, since you'd seen me more often when I served you coffee or drinks at the house, though I confess I'm not convinced that coming here will be any good, as you educated gentry are geese of a feather, and will always flock together.

You know how generous Niño Ubaldino used to be to everybody, and I know it won't come as a surprise if I tell you that before he died he promised Néstor and me the balconied cottage at the back of the garden. Shortly after Niño's death Doña Laura agreed to keep his pledge, and swore on her part that, when she passed away, the house would be ours, as she's always been very respectful of the deceased's last word. And so we've waited patiently for five years for it to come about, and now that Doña Laura is gravely ill our expectations are naturally higher than ever. But recent events at the house have made us fear we'll be cheated out of our inheritance, Don Hermenegildo, and this time we're not going to let the fox run away with the chickens, no sir, we're not going to let him steal our bird.

It's as though I could still see them when they all rushed out of the house the day of their father's funeral, the four sisters with their husbands in tow and Arístides bustling after them, crying at the top of their voices as they stumbled down the stairs that they'd never set foot in the house again after the injustice done to them, trampling the pink begonias and treading on the myrtle bushes that bloomed on the path that went up to the house, stepping into their black limousines and angrily slamming the doors shut so that Doña Laura would hear them, poor lady, who couldn't hear anything by that time, half-fainted and trembling as she lay in Gloria's arms. It's as though I could still see them, yes sir, the four sisters and their brigand brother, tearing their hair out by the roots as they leaned over the open coffin, scratching their cheeks and their foreheads as they called out for justice, their father still laid out in his silk-lined casket and staring at them with that tranquil gaze that he never had while he was alive because his family was always driving him crazy, but that had spread now over his face like a balm as death slowly spread its mantle over him. Because nobody has died a sudden death in that house, Don Hermenegildo, they've all died bit by bit, long before they're apparently dead.

Néstor and I can tell you about it in detail. For example, the way we've been ordered to set the table every night these five years, placing Niño Ubaldino's plate as usual at the head of the table, as though he were still alive. It's because we're so painfully aware of his presence that we're both excruciatingly careful when we serve the table: We lift our crystal water pitchers slowly over the ladies' shoulders, lined in purple or raven silk, so as to also pour some in his goblet; we measure the amount of chicken in Madras sauce or of lobster dipped in mayonnaise left at the bottom of the serving dish so that it'll be sufficient for all, so that it will appease the appetite of three supper guests instead of two. It's because of it that, as we pass the trays near his chair, carved with the family's coat of arms, we take scrupulous care not to bend over too close, because the memory of great men, like the presence of ancient trees, will still make itself felt many years after they've been cut down.

So many years of service, Don Hermenegildo, so many years of worrying about Doña Laura simply because on his deathbed he confided her to our care. "Take care of Laurita for me," he pleaded, "don't forsake her when I'm gone." And the price we had to pay for that promise, what it has cost us! You can't imagine how many ladies of Guamaní have driven out here to beg us to work for them, to entice us with their fake Moorish gold, knowing we'd never leave Doña Laura because we'd given our word to a dead man, and it's not right to betray the dead, poor things, since they're left so defenseless. What we came to complain about to you would never have happened if Niño Ubaldino had been alive, we swear, because he was someone you could really trust, and then Titina wouldn't be sitting here, talking to you this very minute.

I call him Niño Ubaldino because he grew up suckling a black woman's milk, yes sir, Ubaldino grew up hanging from our mother's tit, Encarnación Rivera, a freed slave. At times I even ate off of his plate, licked the egg custard that was his favorite dessert from his own silver spoon. You simply have to try this, Titina, so you'll know what a bit of heaven tastes like, so you'll know how much I'll always love you, he'd say. That's the reason we stayed in the house, catering to the family for thirty years for a miser's pay; although of course the cottage in the garden and Ubaldino's promise had always been at the back of our minds.

It was Ubaldino who brought us here in the first place, and for that reason we always thought of ourselves as his personal servants, although it's true that for the last five years we've been strictly under Doña Laura's orders. We've remained with her because of a point of honor, a matter of personal loyalties toward those who entrusted her to us from the grave. But God is our witness that working for Doña Laura is no piece of cake, no sir, it's no bishop's plum pudding. Before we arrived here Ubaldino was going out of his mind because the servants wouldn't last, they couldn't take Doña Laura's peevishness, her constant tantrum fits. He was always driving out to the slums in his oyster-white Pontiac to look for maids and cooks, and not even because it was for him, and everybody loved him so, would they come to the house to work.

So much for the years spent dusting empty lodgings, so much for the beating of rugs and for the spreading of fresh sheets on the bed every night when no one was going to sleep in them, but just in case Zebedea or Eulalia drops in tonight, Titina, or just in case Ofelia or Margarita decides to pay a visit, and knowing all the while that they weren't going to come, that since their father's death five years before not one of them would deign set foot in this house. They'd call her up on the phone, of course, to see how you're doing mother dear, to find out if you're feeling fine today. Because since they heard that their father had cut them out of the will and that their mother had agreed, they call her up to find out if the old lady still hasn't kicked the bucket, if she hasn't given up the ghost. And Margarita is the worst of all, since that one, once she married Don Augusto Arzuaga and went to live in Santa Cruz, neither calls, nor writes, nor visits, but turns her nose up at all of us. Now that she's a millionaire in her own right, she won't let anyone call her Niña anymore but Doña Margarita, and she laughs at the way her family is flying at one another's throat for a few cents.

When Doña Laura woke up today feeling worse than usual, Néstor and I ran to get the doctor, and we brought him to the house this morning. Then we spread Doña Laura's Venetian lace tablecloth, a precious heirloom, on the table, because we were sure they'd all turn up at the house today, yes sir, and sure enough they did. They rang the bell a bit later and walked into the dining room together, chatting all the while and ordering things to drink and to eat as though nothing was happening in the next room. I left them there with Néstor catering to their whims, serving them dessert and coffee on gold-rimmed plates and saucers.

You must excuse my bluntness in this matter, Don Hermenegildo, but I've been working with the family for so many years that I consider myself a part of it. And it's not just my loyalty to Niño Ubaldino that has brought me here, to make sure the wishes of that great man are carried out, but because I also want to make certain that justice is done for Gloria and little Nicolás. They're the ones who should really benefit from Doña Laura's inheritance, because they're the ones who need it most and because it's God's will it should be so. When Nicolás died she stayed here, taking care of Doña Laura day and night, instead of taking off to make her way in the world as a nurse, which she could have easily done. Since Nicolás passed away Doña Laura's only joy has been Nicolasito, that little cherub who fell to us from the clouds to brighten the sadness of two terrible deaths. Nicolasito was born before his grandfather's demise and a few days after his father's airplane accident, and for that reason Doña Laura is very attached to him. But in spite of everything that Gloria has done to help Doña Laura, in spite of having spent all these years keeping her company, you know how people like to gossip about her in town. And simply because she hasn't married again and stays home thinking of her poor dead husband, for whom she's never taken off her mourning weeds, and still cries herself to sleep every night thinking about him. It's enough to see her getting up early in the morning and setting out for mass, with her lavender dress, her lavender bag, and her lavender shoes, to make one's heart tighten with pity, and when it rains or the sun is too strong she opens her lavender umbrella and walks sadly down the edge of the beach until she reaches town. But in Guamaní to be single and walk the streets means you're risking your reputation, and now Arístides and his sisters are spreading the rumor that Gloria is loose with men, may God save her soul, when what they're really after is the money that's coming to her. In the meantime Gloria never even notices what they're up to, lost as she lives in her world of dreams.

The truth is both ladies have been very unlucky these past few years; it makes me want to cry when I think about it. Just look at what happened to Nicolás and then to his father; it's as though one ghost joined hands with the next one, gratefully pulling each other out of this sorrowful world. We poor people never expect anything from life any more, Don Hermenegildo, we're used to staring death in the face. But when a young man like Nicolás, so kind and rich and good-looking, dies such a terrible death, it's something very difficult to come to terms with. If it didn't make me feel like crying, the irony of it all would make me want to laugh. When I remember that fake funeral coming down the mountain, with people carrying hundreds of wreaths wrapped in emerald-green wax paper; the empty coffin swaying this way and that, the priest and the acolytes carrying lighted tapers, dressed in red cassocks muffled with lace as they recited their prayers for the dead; and poor Doña Laura throwing herself on top of the coffin as though Nicolás had been in it, as though there had been something more than just a shoe or a hand, perhaps a bit of hair or a shred of suit, which was all the rescuers had found among the trees in the wood, because that's all that was left of him after the airplane accident. If it really was an accident, Don Hermenegildo, because some of us have our doubts, and suspect that Nicolás was purposefully butchered and thrown to the winds, that someone had planned it all from beginning to end.

I beg you not to misunderstand me; please don't look so appalled at my story. I haven't come here to make false accusations or to add more fuel to the slander that has already let loose a pack of hounds upon the town. The truth is we suspected Nicolás wouldn't live very long, he was too good for this world. His father was wrong when he thought one day he'd make him into a sugar tycoon like himself. Nicolás was only interested in poetry and in doing his neighbor good; like St. Martin, he'd give half his cape to the poor every time he had the chance. That's why they killed him, that's why his plane was crushed on the mountainside like a useless firefly.

Niño Ubaldino was always an honorable man; he'd have let his right hand be cut off before he'd sell a single acre of land to the northerners. "Manifest Destiny," "Big Stick Policy," the "American Army Mule," even "Scott Emulsion," "Palmolive Soap," "Baseball," and that wonderfully quaint invention, the "toothbrush," which the marines brought with them stuck in their hats when they landed on the island, all became hateful words to him, part of the same vocabulary with which he damned the heavens every morning, as he shaved, washed his face, and combed his hair before the mirror I held up to his face. He never could understand why Providence had sent us those pale adventurers, white and cold and vinegared like sliced palmetto hearts, to take away what was ours. When the girls began to grow up and they all married into those families that held shares of Snow White Mills (all except Margarita, of course), Niño Ubaldino became ill and was bedridden for more than a week. It was one thing to dance on the tightrope and scuttle this way and that, defending your lands by hook or by crook, he said, and something else to hand them over on a silver platter, as he complained to me while I shined his boots; it was one thing to invite them to our parties, where they could dance and taste our native food under our starry skies, listening to the guitar, the guiro, and the calabash gourd, he moaned as I brushed the lapels of his white linen suit before he went to work, and something else to serve them a meal out of our own ribs. And when Margarita became engaged to Don Augusto Arzuaga, the industrial tycoon from Santa Cruz, that was the straw that broke the camel's back. Niño Ubaldino had heard a lot about Don Augusto, and that he was a great friend of the northerners. He was famous throughout the island for the ease with which he took them out of his pocket and put them back again, always profiting by them. But Niño Ubaldino didn't admire him for it.

Ubaldino finally got over his depression, and married off his daughters in style. He was present at all the weddings, bought them each a splendid trousseau, silverware, linen tablecloths and sheets, and from the head of the table he went on smiling at them, inviting his sons-in-law to ride with him to the cane fields in the afternoon, where he would pass in review his army of emerald swords. After all, what happened later was to be expected. Ubaldino wasn't just going to let the newcomers take away what it had taken him years to rescue from the wrong hands, as he used to say to me when I poured out his coffee in the morning, because for that purpose Doña Laura had given birth to two sons, Arístides and Nicolás, who were there to fight for our rights. For one must be considerate of the northerners, be a generous host to them, he'd say to me as I handed him his hat and his briefcase, but one must never bed in with them.

And so today they've all come back to the house where Gloria, Néstor, Nicolasito, and I have lived so peacefully these last five years, laughing at Doña Laura's last breath, buzzing like flies around the only brother they've left and hoping he'll help them out. But we know he can't help them because Doña Laura has made up her mind to leave everything she owns to Gloria and Nicolasito. And that's the reason I'm here today, Don Hermenegildo, to tell you we know a will exists because we've seen it with our own eyes, in Doña Laura's handwriting. And if Arístides should make it disappear after Doña Laura's death we'll be left without the cottage at the back of the garden Niño Ubaldino promised us so many years ago. This is why I'm asking you to help us, to come out to the house and ask Doña Laura to give you the deed for safekeeping before she passes away. This time we're not going to let the fox get away with the chickens, no sir, we're not going to let it run away with our bird.

Something extraordinary has happened. Yesterday, as I was sitting in my office, working on my biography of Ubaldino De la Valle, Guamaní's patrician statesman, Titina Rivera, the De la Valles' everlasting maid, came in the office and told me a story that has left me aghast. I'd heard rumors about Gloria Camprubi in town many years ago, but I never paid attention to them as they came from unreliable sources. They'd say that when she first came to the De la Valles' home she was Arístides's lover, and worked there as a nurse helping Laura take care of poor Ubaldino who was so sick at the time; and that later she had married Nicolás, which had caused a family feud. Nicolás's tragic death soon afterward was blamed on the jealousy that tore the brothers apart, although suicide was never actually proven. And now Titina has come with a totally different explanation to those events, suggesting that Nicolás was really murdered by his brother and sisters, in their struggle to keep Diamond Dust for themselves. She added ominously that Laura has made a new will that benefits Gloria and her son, and that she can't answer for what could happen to them. An accusation like that cannot be made publicly without facing the inevitable consequences, and I've decided to pay the De la Valles a visit. I owe it to Ubaldino to try to help his family out, as well as to protect his good name. I never did care much for Arístides or his sisters, and didn't get to know Gloria very well. But I respect Laura, she was always a good wife and mother. Every family in Guamaní hides a skeleton in the cupboard and Ubaldino's family is probably no different. But it's better to forget these unhappy events, erasing them with the edifying accounts of his heroic exploits. Every country that aspires to become a nation needs its heroes, its eminent civic and moral leaders, and if it doesn't have them, it's our duty to invent them. Fortunately this is not the case with Ubaldino, who was truly a paragon of chivalrous virtue, and whose story I have already begun to relate in my book. I think it's befitting that I should visit the De la Valles' home today. This way I'll pay my last respects to Laura and see if I can be of help in the matter of the will. The sight of Titina, whom I hadn't seen for years, left a deep impression on me. She hasn't changed at all. She must be at least seventy-five years old, but her hair is jet black as ever, not a single silver ringlet to sadden her temples. Titina, the De la Valles' immortal servant, Guamaní's last slave; Titina, the timeless one.

IV.

DON JULIO'S DISENCHANTMENT

"AFTER DOÑA ELVIRA'S TRAGIC DEATH, DON JULIO FONT was visited by a host of troubles. A number of powerful banks from the north had recently opened branches in Guamaní, and their red granite palaces flanked by white stucco lions were the new sensation in town. These banks, however, found no difficulty in financing the new sugar corporations that had recently arrived in town, but mistrusted island initiative. For this reason, the Portalatinis, the Iturbides, and the Plazuelas, owners of such renowned sugar mills as Toa, Cambalache, and Eureka, who had until then worn the titles of their plantations like bejeweled coronets of duchies or marquisates, had recently seen their concerns tumble into the abyss of ruin. They had been forced to sell a great deal of their lands in order to finance their new crops, and they no longer had enough volume of cane to make their businesses profitable ventures. Don Julio had sworn that Diamond Dust would not share the same fate, and he had refused to sell to the newcomers a single acre of cane.

He had been a dry goods merchant for many years, and thus had many friends in the circle of Spanish bankers of the island's capital. These natives of Spain considered themselves adoptive sons of America, and had had in the past provided Diamond Dust with ample financial support. They trusted Don Julio, as well as the criollo landowners, and had a profitable business with them that had lasted many years. But the arrival of the new banking institutions from the north, as well as the new official credit control in dollars, had forced them out of business, and many had decided to leave the island for good. For the past few years, Don Julio had heroically financed his sugar production himself, because he saw that his friends were no longer well off and would not easily be able to help him. The day finally arrived, however, when the last bag of gold that he had stacked in the cellar finally vanished, and he decided to pay a visit to Don Rodobaldo Ramírez, his oldtime friend and president of the by then defunct Bank of Bilbao. He found him taking down the Victorian mirrors of his living room and selling his carved consoles and rocking chairs to the highest bidder, with his mind made up to sail from the island with his family.

'You're just a bunch of traitors, you lousy no good Spaniards,' he told his friend half in jest, half in ire, while he gave a hand with the luggage and helped carry the heavy trunks aboard the freighter *Borinquen*. 'What God has joined in heaven may no man rend asunder on earth, and our destiny will be bound forever more to this island's tragic fate.'

Don Rodobaldo looked at him sadly, from under the snowy scorpions of his eyebrows. They had been born in the same town and had made the crossing to America together; later they had shared countless *cazuelas* of beef tripe and sizzling codfish in parsley and garlic sauce, while they reminisced about their hometown and sang the beauties of the golden wheat fields of Lérida.

'Sorry, Chano, old friend,' he answered calmly, calling Don Julio by the same name he had known him by since childhood. 'You know the saying, "An old Moor will make a bad Christian," and at my age I'd be afraid to become organi-

cally different.' Don Rodobaldo was referring to the new
governor's frenzied campaign to Americanize the island, just
a few months before the passing of the Jones Act into law.

'You can always change your mind later on,' Don Julio
told him. 'Right now you must stay and help me out. Just
give me a year, lend me the money I need to finance the
seeding of my new crops, and as soon as our legislature is
allowed to meet again, all our problems will be solved.'

Don Rodobaldo looked at him and shook his head sadly.
'They may name some of our citizens to the senate and to the
chamber of deputies,' he said, 'but everything will stay the
same. From now on it's the Americans who'll have the last
word, even when the Puerto Ricans are allowed to govern,
and I'm too old to molt my feathers.'

The *Borinquen* sailed that very afternoon, fading away like
a small brightly lighted city past the dark coves of El Morro
Bay. Crestfallen and despondent, Don Julio went back to
Guamaní the following day. He felt his last friend had abandoned him, and that he was now alone in the world. A few
days after this mournful farewell, another sort of misfortune
came upon him. The invitation to the inauguration of Snow
White Sugar Mills, the ultramodern refining complex the
newcomers had been building for months on the valley, had
finally arrived in the mail.

Up and down the prairies of Guamaní had run rumors that
the newcomers had declared a ceasefire in the war of the
sugar mills, and that they were now anxious to help out the
criollo hacienda owners, sharing with them their marvelous
new contrivances. When Don Julio found out about these
rumors, he thought he had come to the end of his troubles,
and he decided to attend the celebrations, persuaded that
during all the hobnobbing and socializing he could bring
about the scheme he had thought up concerning the owners
of Snow White Mills.

On the day of the inauguration the sun was shining like a
gold doubloon. High up in the sky, through ruffled clouds
that fluttered like guajana feathers whisked by brisk Alisio
winds, a huge silver zeppelin could be seen sliding over the
valley of Guamaní, supervising the feverish activities that had

begun to take place below at early dawn. The zeppelin had been rented by the inaugural committee, and it came and went over the cane fields dragging after it a long tail of red, white, and blue banners. 'April 15, 1918—Follow our Example,' proclaimed the flaming streamers every time they were spread out by the wind, as the zeppelin pointed its blunt nose toward the new mill.

The airship was meant to signal the way to the festivities' fun grounds, so that the numerous guests who were expected from Ensenada Honda could easily find their way to them. The inaugural committee had sent out telegrams to all the neighboring haciendas, inviting them to send their delegates to join in the revelries, and Don Julio, who was by then president of Diamond Dust, had been among them. Riding his chestnut mare, he had joined the lively caravan of two-wheeled light chaises, sulkies, and hansoms that that morning could be seen headed toward the new mill. He felt happy and lighthearted, convinced that it was to be a great day for Diamond Dust, and, like everybody else in Guamaní, piqued by curiosity as to what he would see there. The holiday atmosphere, the smiling faces of the sugar mill owners who galloped by his side on their spirited steeds toward Snow White Mills, had lifted all foreboding and made him retrieve his old confidence in the future of the island.

Once he reached the fair grounds, he made his way among the jostling crowds, ignoring the looks of hate his old friends, the criollo hacienda owners of Guamaní, gave him. Most of them refused to speak to him since Doña Elvira's death, because they blamed him for her tragic end. He walked with shoulders proudly erect, swaggering among the local gentry and taking advantage of his conspicuous height to dominate the scene. The afternoon's entertainment had been entrusted to the cadets of the Marine Corps who, outfitted in their gala uniforms, with white leggings and burnished caps gleaming in the noonday sun, blew their tubas and rolled their drums, clashed their cymbals and puffed on their trumpets, as they sat on the gaily festooned bandstand. There were so many of them they would take turns in their different duties, and when they didn't play in the band they ladled the punch, passed the trays of hors d'oeuvres among the guests, and waltzed the daughters of the criollo landowners around in their arms. Don Julio strolled over to the punch bowl and, making an effort, managed to down a cup of purple Tipperary, spiced with tea and wine. He couldn't understand why the newcomers liked such vile stuff, when all around them grew some of the most luscious cane fields in the world, and at the heart of each blade of sugar lay hidden a golden staff of rum. Don Julio, like the rest of the criollo hacienda owners of the valley, never drank anything but rum, which they had for centuries distilled themselves in rustic copper wires. He then walked on to the warehouse, where the new mill's equipment was displayed. The engines had been greased and burnished for the occasion, and they shone on their cement pedestals like splendid, exotic insects that no one there had ever seen before. Instead of the old vertical steam mills, equipped with their slow-balance wheels and oscillating iron beams, which he had with such difficulty brought over from France for Diamond Dust many years ago, the new mill had horizontal grinders, with compact steel wheels and swift winches; instead of the coarse wooden troughs, where his field hands used to shovel molasses patiently for days, they had breathlessly whirling centrifugal drums, which did the same job in seconds; and his rudimentary Jamaican train, a series of huge iron vats in which cane juice had been slowly boiled for centuries, now seemed to him a picturesque antique, a quaint collector's item next to the new mill's multiple evaporators and its miraculous vacuum pans, which would magically work on their own and needed no human supervision. Open-mouthed and with eyes shining greedily like new Spanish *escudos*, he saw how the multiple evaporators worked, as they turned the sugarcane juices into molasses, when a handful of sugar crystals was introduced into the vats, so that the huge cylinders of boiling liquid would instantly be filled with Snow White sugar.

Don Julio saw Mr. Durham, the president of the mills, sitting at the platform for honored guests, and drew near to pay his respects. Next to Mr. Durham sat Mr. Irving, the president of the National City Bank, and as he approached

them he couldn't help listening to their conversation. 'With
our modern engines the company will soon be turning out
sixty tons of sugar a year, way over what all the mills of the
local gentry put together can produce,' said Mr. Durham.

Don Julio was amazed at what he had heard, but he
pretended not to be. He greeted both men with a polite
smile. 'I'm your neighbor, Don Julio Font,' he said to Mr.
Durham. 'I've come to put myself at your service.' Mr.
Durham blinked several times before he recognized him.

'Of course, now I remember!' he said, looking surprised.
'You're the landowner next to us, the one with the priceless
cane fields!' But, in spite of the subtle jeer, he shook his hand
cordially.

'Maybe he's changed his mind,' interposed Mr. Irving, also
greeting Don Julio, whom he knew by sight. 'We'll need all
the help we can get from the natives to make Snow White a
success. And not just for the sake of the Caribbean, but for
the progress of the world.' Mr. Irving was a well-bred white-
haired gentleman, and his cordiality contrasted greatly with
Mr. Durham's stiff-necked pomposity.

Don Julio told himself he shouldn't mention the subject he
had come to speak of straightaway, and he kept silent a few
moments, good-naturedly observing the spectacle below with
a benign expression on his face. The band was playing full
swing, and a company of uniformed cadets was marching in
perfect formation before them, twirling their silver batons to
the rhythms of John Philip Sousa's 'Semper Fidelis.' There
were flags displayed everywhere: they trembled like bee's
wings on the ropes that were draped as a railing around the
grandstand, they hung in tricolored festoons on the new
machinery, they were even stamped in Philadelphia Cream
Cheese on all the sandwich trays the marines were passing
among the guests.

'It makes you think of an invading army, doesn't it?' Don
Julio told Mr. Durham innocently, pointing toward the squad-
ron of battleships that could be seen gleaming in the distant bay
of Ensenada Honda, and on whose steel turrets quivered
thousands of banners under the noonday sun.

'It doesn't make you think of an army, it *is* an army,' Mr.

Durham answered, looking bemused. 'Twenty years ago it brought you freedom and order; this time it's bringing you our nation's progress. Thanks to that army out there your island is being inaugurated today into the modern age.'

All of a sudden Don Julio felt uncomfortable, and he loosened the tie around his neck, to find some relief from the heat. 'And what exactly do you mean by that?' he asked in a slightly ruffled tone, frowning for the first time at his host. 'Do you mean that under Spanish rule there was no progress on our island?'

Mr. Irving had taken off his white cotton gloves and was fanning his perspiring face with the wing of his top hat. 'Please don't be upset, Don Julio, it's much too hot for that. Mr. Durham only meant that we had brought to your island the progress of the twentieth century. The progress of the nineteenth century undoubtedly belongs to you.'

Don Julio nodded silently, and accepted Mr. Irving's subtle apology. He rose from his seat and took a deep breath, so that he towered above both his listeners. His chest had widened considerably in the last few years, and his old white linen suit, which was now too tight for him, had become inordinately creased and soggy. But he still cut an imposing figure next to Mr. Durham and Mr. Irving, who were dressed in black cutaways with swallow tails. 'There's really very little difference between your type of a protectorate and ours,' he said in a conciliatory tone. 'I totally agree with you that a country as small as this one can't be without a mentor; and Spain, our mother country, was the great protector of the derelict nations of this continent, all through the nineteenth century. Your country is to be admired, because it's doing the same thing today. For this reason I wish to arrive at a business agreement with Snow White Mills.' And he explained to Mr. Durham that he was willing to sell him some of his cane fields, if he would persuade Mr. Irving and the bank to lend him the money he needed to modernize his own mill.

'Please don't get me wrong,' he added, laughing, as he looked first one man, and then the other, straight in the eye. 'I don't want you to take me for a criollo hacienda owner, with a rundown mill no bigger than an olive press. I own a full-sized business, and I don't intend to mortgage my assets to kingdom come. If I've made up my mind to sell, it's because the loan from the City Bank must be big enough to turn Diamond Dust someday into Snow White's legitimate rival.' He had spoken in jest, with a cajoling lilt to his voice, convinced that he'd been paying them a compliment. Dumbstruck in the granite wool of his cutaway, Mr. Irving stared aghast at Don Julio. Suddenly he burst out laughing.

'So that's it!' he said to Mr. Durham. 'This man thinks our bank is Snow White's business partner! I'm afraid you're mistaken, my friend. We've no vested interests whatsoever in this venture, and there's no way Mr. Durham can tell us what to do.' And taking Don Julio gently by the arm, he explained that his bank's role was not to choose between criollo and foreign landowners, but to loan out money to solid enterprise, for the good of all.

Don Julio turned around slowly, as an armored ship will lean toward starboard when about to meet the enemy head on. He stared at Mr. Irving incredulously. 'Are you implying it's not true? That you don't make loan exceptions with northerners?' he answered tartly, throwing all caution to the wind. 'What do you take me for, a gullible country dolt, or a Spanish simpleton? It's no news to anyone here today that this whole show has been financed by you!' And rising abruptly from his chair, he stepped down in a rage from the grandstand, furiously elbowing his way through the crowd.

Snow White's inauguration was a huge success. In just one afternoon its owners had met most of the patrician upper crust of Guamaní, so that now they could call one another familiarly by their first names. The next day, however, the lively caravan of chaises, sulkies, and hansoms took off in the opposite direction to the mill, and headed toward town. Heartened by the warm reception they had been given at Snow White Mills, and galvanized into action by the marvels they had seen there, every criollo hacienda owner, every proprietor of a twobit grinder or sugarcane crusher, had recovered his lost hopes as to the future of his own business. Their appetites whetted, they swept like hawks into Guamaní

and milled in a clamoring mob in front of the First National
City Bank, demanding that they be given the same financial
privileges as the northern investors. On that day, however,
they received their second lesson in military science. Standing at attention before the red granite gates of the bank, with
their rifles slung on their backs like fixed angel's wings, and
outfitted in the same gold-buttoned navy-blue gala uniforms
that had made their daughters swoon just the evening before,
were the cadets of the Marine Corps, fiercely barring their
way."

V.

THE CONFESSION

I'M DEEPLY GRATEFUL FOR YOUR VISIT, DON HERMENEGILDO. I'll never forget you came to mourn with us this afternoon when the rain and the tears are equally flooding our hearts, when the winds have smitten the four corners of this house, so that now it will be forever despoiled by grief. What Titina told you in your office is true: Mother has been agonizing since yesterday. Her passing on, however, will not be anything extraordinary; we see it as a smeared, bespattered copy of a greater tragedy, our father's foreboding demise five years ago, when our dignity was rent to shreds.

Yes, the document you've come to talk to us about exists, friend, no doubt about it. I'll make sure to tear it up with my own hands when our mother finally comes to rest. I give you my word that that scheming, ambitious hussy won't be making a farce out of justice at Diamond Dust Sugar Mills, no sir, we won't let her let loose her pack of lies upon the town, trying her best to ruin us, to throw her insults at us. Yes, it's also true that when Mother has finally gone the way of all

35

flesh and this annoying matter of the will has been cleared up, I plan to sell Diamond Dust to my brothers-in-law, the owners of Snow White Mills. Don't stare angrily at me like that, Don Hermenegildo, as though I were a traitor to our country. I've read your impassioned novels in which you vindicate our national rights, and I beg you to listen patiently to my story before you make up your mind to damn me for my actions. I feel sure that, once you've heard it, you'll come to understand my wish not only to sell Diamond Dust, but to banish the memory of this house, of this town, and of this valley and go to live in the capital, where no news of our dishonor or of our shame has as yet arrived.

You probably think it's unusual that my sisters and I should all be sitting around the dining-room table instead of going into Mother's room and standing next to her bed as she breathes her last, so as to comfort her in her agony. The reason we haven't done so is that Gloria Camprubí, our sister-in-law, is in there with her, and it wouldn't be at all seemly if we were to share Mother's death with her. But it really doesn't change things, because even sitting out here we're witnesses to her suffering. We don't need to enter the room to see Mother hardly breathing, laid out in all her finery upon the Madeira lace pillows, the contours of her body leaving hardly an imprint on the deep feather mattress, surrounded by the ebony pillars of her canopied bed as by four ghostly sentries who watch over her dreams.

We need only close our eyes and we can see Gloria sitting next to Mother, handkerchief to her eyes and elbow propped on the night table, anxiously leaning her heavy body over the mess of medicine bottles, used needles, and stained cotton balls; a scene that immediately convinces us of her guilt in all this affair from its beginnings. You'd only have to look at her closely, as I've done hundreds of times, to discover on her face traces of that sadness she has touted high and low over the years and which she smears over her eyes in thick dabs of kohl, spreading its purple oiled wings in deep shadows under the sockets of her eyes to adorn her mourning, to proclaim herself the faithful defender of her husband's good faith while all the time she's secretly yearning for me. You'd only need to reach out and touch her face, feeling out the thick crust of makeup that she has spread over her cheeks and forehead, to graze with the tips of your fingers the cheap earrings made of purple plastic balls that bob garishly next to her smile, the wrinkled, faded silk anemones that she tucks provocatively between her breasts or in her hair, to know that she's demented, hopelessly out of her mind. You'd only have to do this once, I swear, to understand in advance everything I'm going to tell you, to comprehend why it's inconceivable that any courtroom on earth today should name Gloria Camprubí the legal heiress of Diamond Dust Sugar Mills.

My sisters and I have been sitting around this table for hours, Don Hermenegildo, waiting for the inevitable outcome. Only Nicolás is missing, poor boy, still dreaming of the whims of the just under the marble angel carved in his image and likeness Mother had made in Italy to stand over his tomb in Guamaní's graveyard, next to the sea. Among the five of us we've already taken care of the funerary details: we drew up the mortuary notes for the press, we ordered a rented limousine that will carry her mortal remains to the cemetery, we ordered the silver shroud, heavy with white orchids, which will mantle her coffin with the dignity due to her station. And now you've come to join us, offering to help us carry its saddening pall on your shoulders.

My father's death taught us a terrible thing, Don Hermenegildo: our love for the dead, like a floating iceberg, can only be measured by the depths of our resentments. On the surface everything's normal, we sail merrily on, all hands on deck and banners flying, but with time the memory of the hurts we once suffered because of someone's cruelty begins to grab at us like the hand of a drowning man struggling vainly to reach the surface. We then begin to think about everything that we, because of modesty and self-respect, have kept to ourselves and never complained about when they were still alive, and those truths begin to fester at the bottom of our hearts, forming slowly suppurating sores of hate or, what is even worse, wounds that drain from us the blood of love. We who are still alive must then begin to rid ourselves of our beloved dead, lending a deaf ear to their pathetic snapping and gnashing of teeth; we must attempt to forget them, pushing them tenderly to one side or tearing their embraces of ice away from us as they attempt to press us desperately to their bosom, to drag us down with them to the depths of oblivion. The truth is the dead can't live without us, Don Hermenegildo, they take their nourishment and the air they breathe from our innermost thoughts. We all have one or two of our dead put away in this way in the secret cupboard of our souls; friends and acquaintances we once loved deeply but who wouldn't love us back, who were too jealous or mistrustful to accept our affection, our sincere will to share with them the bounties of life. These beloved dead, although painful, are in fact easy to forget, and we sit them unceremoniously on the shelves of our memory as if they were dolls filled with sawdust and wadding. But when the dead are closer to us, Don Hermenegildo, when it's a matter of a father or a brother, for example, the pain we feel when we stumble upon them on our sleepless nights as we falter down a dark corridor is much deeper, and it can threaten us like a yawning abyss. Such is my case at the moment, and I confess that since my brother's death five years ago I've lived in hell, a hell that tightened its flames around me three months later when it was Father's turn. Neither my father nor my brother ever wanted to love me, Don Hermenegildo, and now it's my turn to pay them back in kind. That's why I'm going to sell Diamond Dust Sugar Mills to my in-laws and tear Mother's testament to shreds as soon as she stops breathing and I can go into her room, my friend, because it's the only way to rid myself of the memory of the hurt.

I was the first to meet Gloria, more than ten years ago, when I was still studying to be an agronomist at the university of the capital. Nicolás was in France at the time, studying literature and philosophy. As he was the firstborn and would some day inherit the presidency of Diamond Dust Mills, no education this side of the Atlantic was good enough for him. Once, when money was tight, Mother pawned her jewelry to pay for his ticket on the *Queen Mary*, so that he would be able to make the voyage back in style. As I was the sensible, pragmatic second son, I was sent to study agriculture at the university, because even though my education wouldn't add any luster to the flourish of the family surname, my skills would one day be needed for an efficient operation of the sugar mill. Such flagrant preferences didn't bother me at the time; I was used to my family's extravagances and found them picturesque to a certain extent, adding an additional flavor to their eccentricities. As you may remember, in his youth Don Julio De la Valle, our grandfather, had once been captain of the small cruiser *Ponce de León*, when he had recently arrived from Lérida to discharge his military duties on the island. The *Ponce* was the only Spanish bathtub to stand firm before the *Terror* and the *Yosemite*, both armed to the teeth with four-inch cannons, during the bombardment of El Morro Castle by the marines in 1898. The *Yosemite* couldn't believe that such a quaint old craft should dare fire its Nordenfeld guns so indiscriminately against a ship more than three times its size, and it mistook the *Ponce* for a torpedo carrier, veering to stern and refusing to engage in combat. Probably at the same time Don Bon Bon Latoni, Mother's father, had joined the invading troops in front of Guamaní's plaza, showing them where the Spanish soldiers kept their wind instruments, and joining them immediately in dancing the jig and playing "There's a Hot Time in the Old Town Tonight," which became the army's national hymn during the rest of the hot and dusty campaign. He became one of the main providers of food and supplies when the troops crossed the island and marched toward the north. It was exploits like these taking place in the same family that made them so cheerfully eccentric; different in a certain sense from the rest of the families of the town, always ready to break the laws of custom and decorum for a dashing heroic deed. And at the time I thought that my having to study the science of agriculture at the university was part of this plan, it was my family's strange way of training me to be a different type of hero, a man in full possession of his capabilities, who would later be able to make his way successfully in the world. As I have always been a practical man, a firm believer in the theory of the survival of the fittest, I accepted my family's design without complaint. I have also, for this same reason, later tried to reach a middle-of-the-road understanding with our powerful neighbors from Snow White Sugar Mills, offering them as you might say the leg of the chicken so that we might enjoy the breast, and letting them have for a pittance the briny, barren lands that stood adjacent to our holdings and which we didn't really need. While Nicolás read Montaigne, Kant, and Hegel in French, dressed in his shiny top hat and tails and promenading himself along the carefree cafés of the Champs Elysées, I learned to speak English without an accent at our university and became imbued in the ancient skills of the land. I lived austerely; lodged in a dilapidated boarding house; studied by the light of a gas lamp and hoarded every penny left over from my food and book expenses in a tin can on whose lid I had written, in large red letters, the maxim "Vade Retro," to discourage myself from embezzling it.

"If suffering will not kill you," a popular saying of ours has it (Nicolás would say it was Nietzsche), "it will make you fatter," and thus I welcomed these torments as worthy of my surname. I was convinced that through them I was to gain the resiliency and ruggedness of character that would one day permit me to save Diamond Dust from ruin. I suspected at the time that once Mother and Father were gone the mill's future would depend on me, and I was right about it, as my decisions have been crucially important these last five years I've been president. No one on the mainland was willing to pay thirty cents a kilo for Diamond Dust Sugar when our neighbor's Snow White sold for fifteen; our product had acquired an aura of luxury, a quaint, old-fashioned brown sugar made by hand, to be served in heirloom porcelain coffee sets. The secret of the business, as I learned at school, was modernization, frugality, and friendship: becoming an ally of our American neighbors. For this reason I studied English assiduously, until I learned by heart the names of all the machinery at the mill in that barbarous tongue. My efforts finally began to pay off when I began to dream in English.

I was a good student and I knew it; and then one day my happiness was complete when I met Gloria Camprubí at the

university, one of those mulatto beauties who are used to
stopping traffic. She led a carefree life then; didn't know
what she wanted and didn't much care. She had been born in
a suburb of Guamaní, her parents owned a small cane farm,
but with the falling prices of sugar they couldn't compete
with production costs and they first sublet and later sold the
property to my father. Her parents had died, she had decided to go to nursing school and lived from day to day,
paying for her studies with the last of her inheritance. When
I met her my life changed drastically; as Saint Paul said,
when you itch it's best to scratch, and so she moved in with
me and kept house, becoming quiet and demure, eager to
please me in every way. When I graduated from the university I took her home with me. My three eldest sisters had
made excellent matches, marrying the sons of Snow White
stockholders, and Margarita, the youngest, had married Don
Augusto Arzuaga, the industrial magnate from Santa Cruz.
The house had become empty, Nicolás was still in Europe
and Mother was feeling lonely. The timing was perfect
to hire the services of a gay, well-behaved young girl
from a family come upon hard times who would keep her
company and help her take care of Father, who was by then
already ill.

Those first six months after Gloria's arrival were the happiest of my life. No sooner had she begun sunning herself on
the balconied galleries that gave on to the cane fields and the
sea, or bathing naked in the rain that rushed out of the sluices
as it drained from the gabled ceilings, than a change came
over the house. We all seemed to be breathing more easily,
refreshed by the breezes that her body set in motion as she
swung her hips down the blue shuttered corridors of the
house, or as she lay like an oak-carved idol under the breathing mosquito net, lulled by the slow soft paddling of the
ceiling fan at the hour of the siesta. Mother was especially
pleased with her, and they would spend hours together picking flowers from the garden and arranging them in iridescent
glass vases. She liked to be read to, and so she would ask
Gloria to read episodes of *Maria*, Jorge Isaacs's novel, out
loud. She used to laugh her head off at its maudlin sentimen-

tality, finding the story of Maria's shorn tresses and bashful kisses, of her sad roses pressed between the pages of a yellowed letter, in the utmost bad taste, the result of a romantic derangement that had finally ruined Efrain. They both patiently took care of Father, who on his part felt so happy at having Gloria at his side that he recovered his long-lost appetite and his good mood. He seemed finally to be reconciled to the fact of growing old. His arteriosclerosis was advancing dangerously, as the doctors had diagnosed, and his circulatory system would one day inevitably crystallize into a shrub of salt.

Meanwhile, I worked myself to death during daytime for the family's sake, but I didn't make any complaints. Nighttime was mine to do as I liked, and nobody seemed to care what I did then. When the lights of the house went out and the old rooster and hens had flown up the tree, I went silently down to the cellar, where mother had fixed a small apartment for Gloria. Those nightly visits made me feel a beatitude I had never experienced before. At dawn after I left Gloria, I'd open the doors of the balcony and look out on the sapphire sea that glittered behind the cane fields, at the cane fields themselves, crested with wave upon wave of silvery plumes as far as the eye could see, at the glinting spurs of the cocks crowing on the crowns of the palm trees, at the velvet green hills that rolled and dipped into each other like the breasts of a woman in love. And taking a deep breath, I filled my lungs with the pure air of my island, agreeing, as I did so, with Don Francisco Oller, who said Puerto Rico was not a land but a landscape, and I understood perfectly why he had given up the glories of Paris and his impressionist friends to come and paint the beauties of his homeland, so that it would be made timeless. At that moment I felt in total harmony with the universe, ready to pardon any future injustice the world or my family may have in store for me. I knew then I not only had the guts to help a cow give birth to its heifer, grabbing it by the tail and pulling it out of the uterus all blue and shiny and ready to be tenderly licked by its mother, I could also hide my rough, worker's hands and my broken nails in my pockets, dress up in fine clothes, and

saunter downtown to ask the American bankers for a new
loan for Diamond Dust, glibly reminding them of my sisters'
connections with some of their most powerful stockholders. I
learned then that, when money is in sight, there are no bonds
of blood, no liens of kin that will hold, and the decision to
divide a profit has the same cruel ring to it as a sinking ship's
cry of "every man for himself." As an example of one of the
most heartless measures I've had to carry out in recent years,
I ordered many of our cane laborers, who I suspected were
illegitimate sons of our father, to be fired unceremoniously.
They were easy to recognize because they all looked vaguely
like him, except duskier in skin and sullen in countenance,
because of their hawk-bridged noses, raging bull's necks, and
barrel chests. In this way I freed the company of a number of
unnecessary expenses, as Father had always insisted on clandestinely taking care of their families, and cut the risks of a
claim to our inheritance down to a minimun. I finally managed, cutting corners here and there and pulling the meager
strings available to me, to make my dreams of modernizing
Diamond Dust come true. With the money I saved I bought
two new tractors and an electric generator, so that my multiple evaporators became the envy of the valley. The mill soon
doubled production, and I managed to pay off the debt that
had been bleeding us like a perforated ulcer these last ten
years. Only one thing worried me at the time and hung like a
dark cloud over the horizon: in spite of my gentlemanly
wooing and courting, Gloria had refused to marry me.

Nicolás returned home that same year. He arrived on
Christmas Eve loaded with presents, and for a while our
house resembled a Paris boutique stinking of expensive perfumes and trinkets. He gave Mother the largest bottle of Joy
on the market, claiming it was good for the soul because it
was distilled from the skin of lovers on their first night of
love, when their sweat had the odor of jasmine and orange
blossoms, and that she should therefore wear it every day as
proof that she was still capable of loving and being loved. He
gave Gloria a sandalwood fan inscribed with a poem in
Chinese, half of which read "I travel through your fingers as
a perfumed river, and my heart beats to the rhythm of your

wrist," but he refused to translate the rest of it, because he claimed its magic wouldn't work if its message was completely deciphered by its user. He gave Titina a huge jar of verbena bath salts and almond oil, which she in turn immediately stashed away in the family cupboard to be used by everyone in the house. But he brought Father the most splendid present of all, an eighteenth-century map of the island drawn by the French naturalist André Pierre Ledrú, in which he traced Juan Ponce de León's daring voyage to the lands of Bimini. Ponce de León had been the first governor of the island, and he had already subdued Agueybaná and Urayoán, built a magnificent house for himself in Caparra, our first town, and married off his three daughters when some Indians came to him and insidiously whispered in his ear the existence of a fountain of youth to the north, where a man could recover his virility with admirable ease. Ponce, who was already old and frail, fell prey to their trap, and immediately set sail toward Bimini, which he baptized Florida. "But he found death instead of youth!" Gloria protested innocently as she curiously examined the parchment, ignorant at the time of the malicious aspects of such a splendid gift.

In spite of these initial demonstrations of civility, it didn't take Nicolás very long to return to his old foolhardy self, swindling his neighbors right and left and blackening our reputation as of yore. He was a rash, indiscreet young man, true to those dreams that Titina has told you about, but never doing anything about them. As a child he always thought himself a hero, and in the home theater scenes we used to set up for the servants on Christmas Eve, he always chose the part of Prince Mishkin, while I acted out the part of the pragmatic Rogozin. When he came back from Europe he was more set than ever on winning over the admiration of our field hands and workers, in spite of the fact that they could hardly understand a word of what such a prince clad in a white silk ruffled shirt and black tuxedo pants, recently emigrated from the Rue de Rivoli into the stinking inferno of the cane field, had to say to them. He insisted they should have decent lodgings instead of living in the old remodeled slave quarters, and began to segregate small pieces of land where they were to build their own houses with part of the dividends the next crop would bring; he was set on bringing water from the river in pipes so that they wouldn't have to bathe in the contaminated rivers any longer, where the blue snails poisoned the waters with bile, so that in a few years their livers were mildewed with the delicate blossoms of bilharzia; and he even insisted on bringing them the blessings of electric power, when our workers, poor things, were afraid of it, and much preferred to cook in their traditional way, balancing their cooking pots over burning coals, between three smooth river stones.

But Nicolás didn't bring these blessings to them for nothing, no sir, it wasn't as if those houses were ripe mangos that fell from the trees; those privileges had a price, which our humble but honest workers had never agreed to pay. It took me awhile, Don Hermenegildo, but I finally discovered his secret. One day, during one of my daily overseeing tours of the mill, I once again heard a ditty the workers used to sing before Nicolás's first voyage abroad. At that time I hadn't made a connection between the two, but now the allusion to his foreign fineries made it all the more evident. The ditty went: "His pants are silk and his shirt is lace; before he was known as Seven Beauties, but now he should be named Bereaved." "Bereaved," that was the nickname by which everyone ominously knew the princely firstborn of the De la Valles. Because no one could deny the truth, and under his savior's pose, beneath his airs of deliverer and liberator, he was really a closet queen, a poor degenerate fool who skewered and twisted and danced before their horrified eyes at the first opportunity he had of being alone with them; who doled and measured out the land and the houses he had promised on the basis of who would and who wouldn't, who could be man enough to trade in his dignity for a piece of bread or a brick. And thus he spent his days preaching social justice and his nights prevaricating in the wilderness of the cane fields, claiming to allay the worker's repulsion and ire, since after all there wasn't such a great difference between prayerful and playful, and in life there had to be a healthy balance of both.

Father, who was growing more and more out of contact with reality, never noticed these things, and two months after his return from Europe he named Nicolás president of the mill.

The news of Nicolás's marriage to Gloria was an even heavier blow. Gloria herself never mentioned it, and it was Nicolás who broke the news to me. Mother, who was feeling increasingly harassed by the demands of Father's illness, was afraid that Gloria would leave her job and that she would find herself condemned to the heavy duties of his care; for this reason she had arranged the marriage as an advantageous contract for all. Nicolás was ashamed to tell me about it, but he never could say no to Mother. In his weak, excitable way he tried to justify his action, begging my forgiveness with pale lips and bowed head, and flapping his arms up and down like a drowning bird everytime we met in the hallways.

At first I was utterly bewildered by it all. My brother, a fag, had managed to succeed where I had failed, persuading Gloria to marry him in just a few months! Later on I reasoned that since I knew Nicolás better than anyone, I knew the marriage was a farce and there was no reason for me to be jealous. I decided to talk to Gloria that very night, ready to drain, with all the patience and prudence I could muster, my heavy cup to the dregs. "Are you really going to marry Nicolás?" I asked her later that night, placing my hand tenderly over the silky mound of her sex. "I thought this was my own private Golgotha, my holy Mount of Olives," I joked. "I never suspected there might be a cash register buried in its depths." Gloria was sitting naked on my knees; we had just made love on her iron cot and my remark made her laugh until the tears came to her eyes. "Of course it's my cash register," she answered when she got her breath back, "but you're the only one who knows the magic words that will open it!" And then she began to kiss me and caress me wildly, reproaching me for my absurd jealousy toward a pitiable pansy, who was making his debut that summer among the breeze-waved plumes of our December cane fields.

A few days later, when I approached Mother on the subject, our talk was much less pleasant. You know very well, Don Hermenegildo, that in this house not a pin falls without Mother's consent, and that she governs all our destinies with a steel hand. On that day, however, I had no choice but to face her, because I feared the consequences of her decision would be disastrous. "If you make Gloria marry Nicolás, I swear you'll be sorry. We're human beings, not cattle to breed and harness." Mother was sitting at her desk, as usual, working at her account books, where she kept track of every penny made and spent at the mill. For a moment I thought she hadn't heard me, because her hand kept on inching over the squares of the ledger like an iron knot. "I swear I can't understand you," she finally said without looking up at me. "A legal wife would be a costly acquisition and you wouldn't be able to save your precious money any longer. This way Nicolás will keep her safe for you, and the whole family will profit by her services." And calmly laying down her pen next to the inkwell, she proceeded to explain all the details of her plan: Nicolás had promised not to touch Gloria; the arrangement would last only as long as Father lived, while she needed the help of a nurse; and once he had passed away the marriage would be annulled. Gloria had agreed to all this, counting on Mother's word that she would receive an adequate sum as payment for her services after a number of years. "Then you can marry her, if you still want her and if she'll take you," she added with a thin smile. Mother's words calmed me down somewhat, Don Hermenegildo, although I still felt silently gnawed by suspicion.

On the face of it, however, I had no choice but to approve the settlement. A month later I was best man at the wedding. It was an intimate, quiet affair, with only Mother, Father, Gloria, Nicolás, the priest, and myself present at the church. In contrast to my sisters' weddings, there was no need to spend on a trousseau, lace tablecloths, or silverware, and the bride wore a simple white linen suit. Father, however, couldn't keep himself from spoiling Nicolás as usual, and he gave him a glittering silver Cessna monoplane as a wedding present. Gloria seemed lighthearted, and couldn't keep her eyes off me all through the ceremony. She stared at me mischievously as though keeping a secret, and she reddened when Nicolás put the ring on her finger, as well as when I toasted their happiness, wishing them a fruitful marriage. Her eyes burned like coals under her simple veil and seemed to want to set me on fire.

After the wedding things went on exactly as before. Gloria spent the next morning with Father as usual, giving him his invalid's bath on a rubber sheet spread out on the bed; the afternoon with Mother, reading to her or doing secretarial work; and the night with me, in our cellar boudoir. The fact that she was now Nicolás's wife made me want her even more intensely, and that night we made love as never before. Happiness, strangely enough, began to make me feel guilty. I felt an absurd pity toward my brother, who, in spite of his pompous title of president of Diamond Dust Sugar, had no authority whatsoever at the mill and seemed as uninterested in honor and power as he was in Gloria's more earthly glories.

It was only three months later, Don Hermenegildo, as I was having breakfast one morning at this same table, that I began to suspect there was a hidden aspect to all this affair which I still hadn't grasped, and that rather than my brother's slayer, I had become his victim. In less than a few weeks after the wedding, Nicolás had become a broken man. He stopped shaving and wearing clean shirts, and went around the house with deep circles under his eyes. He spent most of the day in his room writing poetry, and muttering something about a man being like an arrow, or like a rope strung over an abyss, a minotaur with a torero's body, a misjoined monster, part animal, part man, part saint. On the day I mean, he sat in front of me to pour himself some coffee, and I noticed his hand trembled as he did so. He smiled at me bitterly as he said, "Congratulations! We must have all done a good job, because Gloria is pregnant!"

I asked him what he meant, and sat down stupefied. Nicolás had gone to the sideboard for a bottle of brandy, and again drew his chair calmly beside me. "Forget it, brother," he said in a commiserating tone, while he served himself a drink and then served me one also. "You can't touch her again. Father thinks the baby's his and now she'll be off bounds for both of us." I swear I almost killed him, Don Hermenegildo; I must have punched his face a hundred times, I wanted so to disfigure his princely profile. He finally confessed, spitting the words out amid broken teeth and bleeding tongue. Gloria made love to Father every morning, as soon as I left to oversee the cane fields, and he made love to her in the afternoons.

Six months after this ominous scene, Nicolás took off on his Cessna and headed toward the heavily clouded mountain range of the island. There had been severe storm warnings, and the afternoon sky looked as black as a spilled powder keg. You may think what you will: either he lacked the pluck to go on living, to lend his name openly to the monster Gloria was carrying: his father's child and his mother's grand-child, his brother's child and his brother's brother, his son, his brother, and his nephew all in one; or the field workers of Diamond Dust took justice into their own hands and sabo-taged his airplane.

Once Gloria spawned her offspring one primeval night, be it reptile, fish, or fowl, she stayed home to take care of Mother. Father, distraught by Nicolás's death, died less than a year after the crash, leaving behind an unfair will that threatened to rend our family asunder. He never forgave my sisters for marrying strangers, his business rivals to boot, and he therefore made me his sole heir. As to Gloria and her spawn, he never mentioned them in his will, as was to be expected. Once he lost the illusion of recovered youth, pride became heavier than pleasure, and in the months before his death he hardly knew she existed. When she saw she had lost her husband and her two spirited lovers in a matter of weeks, Gloria began her nightly rounds of the bars of Guamaní, where I'm sure you must have seen her often.

Mother's reaction was also to be expected, as she remains the most eccentric member of our family. After these events her face shriveled into a mask, small and bent and spiny, like the steel cap of a bottle. She kept on as before, locking herself up with seven bolts in the house and working from sunup to sundown in the managing of her accounts. She never seemed to mind Gloria's comings and goings from the town at odd hours of the night, and she gave her a copy of her keys so that she'd be free to do as she wanted. She still owns half of the mill, but she's told all of us categorically that after her death she'll bequeath everything to Gloria and Nicolasito. Her decision horrified my sisters; they couldn't understand why she'd do something like that when she knew what was going on between Father and Gloria. But one has to know Mother as I do to guess what's really going on inside her. I have always been able to read her mind, and I know her resentment toward Father is so great, there's such an iceberg of hate sitting on her heart, that she'll do anything she can to hurt him. And she knows that the only way she can do it now is to leave the mill to Gloria; because if the half-demented town whore inherits the mill, in twenty-four hours the banks will foreclose its loans, and Diamond Dust will be ruined. And that would be Mother's perfect revenge, to cause its downfall, so that its name, as well as Father's, should be annihilated from the face of the earth.

I think that perhaps now you can understand better why I believe I have the right to tear up Mother's will, so that only Father's resolution will be enacted. As to selling Diamond Dust to my brothers-in-law, the owners of Snow White, since we're now all part of the same family, it seems the sensible thing to do. This way the business will survive, the workers will keep their jobs, and I'll be able to reimburse my sisters for the unjust treatment they received from Father, letting them have half my shares. My humiliation and dishonor in this matter have been so great, Don Hermenegildo, that I could never go on living in this town. What I want now is to forgive and forget.

Arístides's confession, his disclosure of what was to be the future of Diamond Dust Sugar Mills, wrenched my soul. For almost half a century I had been witness to Ubaldino's heroic efforts to make it an independent, ongoing concern, and it seemed a terrible pity that they should come to naught. The pictures he had drawn of Nicolás as a degenerate fop, and of Ubaldino himself as a sordid, contemptible man wrecked by illness and disillusionment, had left me hopelessly depressed, but I only half believed them. When he was silent I had to close my eyes, but even so the tears welled up under my lids.

His tale had a feverish aura about it that proved contagious. I found myself breathing with difficulty and got up from the table to walk out on the balcony, where I attempted to clear my mind by breathing in the perfumed breeze of the cane field.

VI.

THE RESCUE

M's novel

"UBALDINO DE LA VALLE'S CIVIC APOTHEOSIS CAME ON THE day he rescued Diamond Dust from being blown away by the wind. We had graduated from the university in the same class, and had joined the Union Party a few years before. We both agreed that our island had been a golden tennis ball on metropolitan tennis courts long enough, and that things couldn't go on as they were. If the president owed Mr. Allen a favor for having exterminated the Indians at Fort Beverly, or on the border of Arkansas or Arizona, if he was in debt to Mr. Yager for dragging Iowa, a renegade state, to vote Democratic, the golden tennis ball immediately landed in their courts and we soon had a new governor.

That summer Ubaldino was running for senator, and as a reporter of *The Nation*, our town's liberal newspaper, I was supposed to follow him everywhere. It didn't surprise anyone when I went into progressive politics, since my father is the owner of *The Nation*, but Ubaldino's family has always been conservative. At first I thought his surname was a drawback, and that it would take votes away from him. With the recent sugarcane bonanza, the American bankers had at last freed their loans and had begun to lend money to the local landowners, thus putting a halt to their mill's growing economic rigor mortis. As a result of that policy, the criollo landowners had all become members of the Republican Party, where they labored toward the political assimilation of the island. For this reason Ubaldino was seen by them as a traitor.

The price they had had to pay for the truce had been high: they were permitted to cut and grind their own cane, but all the sugar had to be refined at Snow White's huge centrifugal drums. The local mills had therefore ceased to be independent, and almost all of them had come to be satellites of the supermill, parasitical and impoverished businesses. For this reason the inhabitants of Guamaní had begun to despise those tail-raising, floor-kissing landowners, as well as everyone who belonged to the Republican Party, while Ubaldino's campaign for greater industrial and political emancipation was attracting more and more sympathizers.

Ubaldino faced one truly great stumbling block before his political career could take off. After his mother died his father had taken Rosa, the family cook, as his mistress, and had had three illegitimate children by her. When he passed on, he had left them the better part of Diamond Dust, and had cut Ubaldino out of most of his mother's inheritance. My friend was thus something like a duke without a dukedom, evicted from that land which for centuries had belonged to his family and which alone justified his social and political ascendancy in the town. Ubaldino himself told me the story of how that unfortunate event had taken place. He was still a child when his great-aunts, Doña Emilia and Doña Estefana De la Valle, had driven out to Diamond Dust in their old two-wheeled sulky. They were ushered in by Néstor, and as they walked gingerly down the shadowy hallway where the family portraits were hung, they stopped for a moment before them. There was the portrait of their great-grandfather, who had come from Navarre and who was very devout, so that with the boards of the ship he had sailed on he had built a canopied bed so large that all his grandchildren could be laid out on it to be baptized in public, for which reason he had called it "The De la Valles' Cathedral." They admired once again the portrait of their grandmother, who was famous for miles around for having been against slavery fifty years before it was eradicated. She gave haven in her cellars to all the maroon slaves who fled from the neighboring haciendas, providing them with sturdy canoes so that under cover of night they might sail for Haiti, where slavery had been abolished. They gazed at their own portrait and saw themselves as little girls again, sitting together in a fake rowboat in the photographer's studio, wearing identical sailor suits with white straw hats and banded necklines, diligently rowing over the painted cardboard waves and pointing the way to the lighthouse of Cabo Rojo, where the pirate Cofresí, their ancestor and a renegade who had raided the rich to aid the poor, had defied the Spanish Guardia Civil in many a bloody shootout. And finally they stopped before Elvira's wedding portrait, where she could be seen holding the huge bridal bouquet of lady of the night that they themselves had picked for her from the garden, and whose blossoms came out only after sundown to spread their ghostly perfume. They both kissed it surreptitiously in the dark with tears in their eyes, before going on to the living room where they were to wait for Don Julio.

He walked in a few minutes later, and they were surprised to see the change that had come over him. He looked spent and haggard, his huge frame had lost its massive weight, so that it now reminded them of an empty warehouse that could at any moment be whisked away by the wind. He was deeply tanned, and was wearing dirty overalls and shoes covered with red clay, so that the sisters guessed he had just come in from the fields. All of which contrasted greatly with the memory they had of him as the country gentleman who had wooed Elvira, dressed in a white linen suit, wide-brimmed panama hat, and almond-oiled hands studded with rings. Don Julio sat down gingerly before them in one of the wicker rockers. 'It's always the same story,' he bellowed at them unceremoniously, 'the damned tractor has hit a stone again. If the people here had any sense, like they do in Lérida, every time they hit a stone they'd lift it from the field and drop it at the edge of the farm, so that eventually they'd not only have a fine stone fence around their property, but they'd have a clean meadow to sow seed in, as well.' Emilia and Estefana both laughed at his remark, agreeing politely. Don Julio took up the coffeepot that Titina had set up on a marble-topped table nearby and started to pour out the coffee.

'It's incredible how everything stays the same in the country,' Emilia agreed, looking around her at the polished oak furniture with admiring eyes. 'It's been ten years, but everything's just as before: Elvira's piano, Grandmother's highboy, Great-Grandfather's chime clock, which he brought over with him on the ship from Spain. You've taken wonderful care of everything, Don Julio.' He smiled and handed her a cup, as though innocently unaware of her innuendo.

'Only one thing's changed, Emilia dear,' he said as he passed both sisters the silver bowl filled to the brim with Diamond Dust, so they might serve themselves, 'it's our sugar. It may be just as sweet as before, but it's becoming more and more bitter to harvest. It's amazing the way sugar is made today, with the sweat of us gentleman farmers.' And as he energetically tinkled his spoon against the sides of the cup, spartanly stirring his bitter, unseasoned coffee, he asked them what it was that had brought them out there. Sitting straight as a pair of black silk spindles on their chairs, the sisters then claimed they were worried by the haphazard way that Ubaldino, their niece's son, was being brought up on the farm. There were no elementary schools in the neighborhood, and the tutors whom Don Julio had promised to contract for the child traveled to the countryside only sporadically. Don Julio immediately agreed to their request. 'After all, he's a healthy, blue-blooded De la Valle. I think it's only natural that he should be brought up by you, since you're willing to foot the bill,' he said with a malicious twinkle in his eye. 'You may groom him and spruce him up all you like, but don't bring him back to me afterward, because the silk-stockinged arts of music, drawing, and dancing in which Elvira excelled so much have never been any good around here.'

Ubaldino was at the oxen's drinking trough at that moment, giving his dog a bath, when he heard Titina calling to come up the stairs to the house. He was bespattered with mud from head to toe, and thus presented a sorry spectacle to his father's visitors when he clambered up the steps two at a time and burst into the room with Bengal barking vigorously behind him. The yellow mutt ran up to Aunt Estefana and planted its slushy paws on her skirt, vehemently wagging its tail and leaving an oozing trail on its jet-black silk. Far from being angry, Aunt Estefana smiled her rice-powdered smile, patted its head, and let it rest its muzzle on her lap. 'You're both coming to town with us,' she told Ubaldino blandly, impressed with the boy's resemblance to her dead niece and trying not to let it show, 'You'll have lots of friends there, and Bengal can help us take care of the hungry mice in the house.'

When a few minutes later they were all standing at the top of the stairs, politely shaking hands and insisting that they mustn't let such a long time go by before they saw each other again, Don Julio drew Ubaldino to one side and clasped him tightly to his heart. 'A young steer will only become a bull once it's been weaned from the udder,' he said to him affectionately. 'I'll probably never see you again, but you must never forget you were also the son of Don Julio Font.' And when he saw the boy was about to climb into the carriage, he handed him a silver coffer with his mother's initials engraved on the lid. 'I've kept Elvira's jewels for you all these years,' he said with a disparaging bow that was meant to be graceful. 'It's the only legacy she left in your name, so be sure to make an honorable use of it.'

A few minutes later the sulky drove down the avenue of whitewashed royal palm trees that led from the house to the main road, with Ubaldino sitting between Aunt Emilia and Aunt Estefana. As he clasped the silver coffer to his bare knees he looked back over his shoulder and saw the smiling, sunlit balcony with its fanlike stairway; the bamboo-shaded river curling lazily next to it; the old slave quarters and the wooden crosses of the slave cemetery only a few paces away; the zinc construction where the mill's machinery was kept; the rusty, decayed chimney chute that valiantly flaunted its white, airy plume across the valley; the house itself, which resembled a huge blue-shuttered galleon sweeping over the plain with all sails unfurled; and as he saw it all slowly disappear, sinking under the green waves of the cane fields, a tear of rage fell silently down his cheeks. 'You may not expect me to, but one day I'll be back!' he swore silently to his father. And thus it was that, save a spare amount of shares that Don Julio had put under his name as a gesture of goodwill, to save face before Elvira's friends and the rest of the landowners of Guamaní, Ubaldino was left without the mill and the lands that had belonged to his family for over a century. Aunt Emilia and Aunt Estefana brought him up valiantly by themselves. Bent like two frail old spiders over their embroidery looms, they worked well into the night making lace mantillas or giving piano classes to the well-to-do children of Guamaní, thus paying for his education until he became of age.

The day before the rescue of Diamond Dust I was sitting at the Café La Palma with a cold beer when I saw my friend coming toward me across the plaza. We both liked the place, and we used to go there often to talk about politics and pool together impossible dreams. We liked to hear the Publico drivers screaming out the names of the towns to which they were about to set out, ready to defy the island's magic labyrinth of jagged peaks and mist-covered ravines that, though it was only a hundred miles long by thirty miles wide, it took at least six months to crisscross and a year to drive around; the barking, fleabitten mongrels; the newspaper vendors, the fruit vendors and the beggars all vying for the attention of the passersby. The noise, the heat, and the dirt made us feel at home, far from the antiseptic mania of cleanliness and orderliness that had come lately over most of the town. I made a place for him at the table under a mango tree, where the dark-green shadows of the leaves periodically swept over the red-and-white tablecloth, swept by the afternoon breeze. Ubaldino took out his handkerchief and mopped the sweat that was pouring down his cheeks.

'I have news for you! I heard this morning at the paper

that your half brothers paid a visit to Mr. Durham, the
president of Snow White Mills. They've just signed an option of ten thousand dollars to sell Diamond Dust to them,
and Mr. Durham has twenty-four hours to come up with the
money.'
    Ubaldino looked amazed. 'Are you sure?' he asked.
    'Of course I'm sure. I wrote the press releases myself.
Look here: "Last locally owned mill in Guamaní to fall in the
hands of northern investors"; "Modern Snow White more
resistant to heat than old-fashioned Diamond Dust." It'll all
be on tomorrow's front page. It's going to be a dandy of a
scandal.'
    'Will they sell the whole thing? The mill, the land, the
house?' Ubaldino seemed elated. His eyes became feverish;
his neck, his cheeks trembled with anticipation.
    'Of course they'll sell the whole thing,' I answered. 'They
say the price is settled; thirty thousand dollars.'
    'This time they've done it, friend; they've really put their
foot in it. The best hunter will fail the fox, but this time
they've let a lion loose. Diamond Dust is worth at least ten
times as much.'
    The next day before dawn we drove out toward Snow
White Mills, where we had heard the meeting was going to
take place. It was so dark we could hardly see our faces in the
car. Ubaldino kept whistling a funny tune I'd never heard
before, a *plena* about a company lawyer being eaten up by
sharks at the beach, and every once in a while he'd pat the
pockets of his jacket, as though he wanted to make sure
something important was still in them. I guessed he had
brought with him his shares of Diamond Dust; the day
before we had discussed the whole thing and I had advised
him that, for our campaign's sake, it was better to sell and
not see himself mixed up in a deal that would probably prove
disastrous, because it would bring down public opinion on
the head of Snow White's owners, as well as on his brothers.'
    Suddenly I had a hunch we were doing the wrong thing.
'Don't sell them,' I said to him in the dark. 'Let's turn around
and go back to town.' Ubaldino looked at me without understanding what I meant.

'Don't sell what?' he said, slowing down the car.

'Your shares of Diamond Dust,' I said. 'No one will be the wiser if you keep them; even the Snow White people may not find out about it for months. By then they'll have come up in value; they'll want to get rid of you as a shareholder and you'll be able to sell them for whatever you may want. And we'll be able to use that money for our campaign against the Republican candidate.'

'Forget it, friend,' he answered. 'After we're through here today, the Republican candidate won't stand a chance.'

It was still dark when we arrived at the mill's company town. We guessed the post office was on the right, because we could hear the flag flapping against the iron pole; the bank and jail were on the left. We parked the old Pontiac next to Mr. Durham's office building and we sat there waiting for a while. It had begun to grow light when I saw Ubaldino's half brothers coming down the street, together with his step-mother, Doña Rosa Font. I had made a different picture of them to myself, and felt strangely disappointed when I saw them. They were shabbily dressed; they looked more like field hands than the sons of a landowner. They were moving slowly, obviously because Doña Rosa was in bad health and couldn't walk fast; they silently helped her cross the square and headed in the direction of Mr. Durham's office. Ubaldino buried his head under his hat and hid behind the steering wheel. A few minutes later we saw Mr. Durham's black Packard drive up the street. Mr. Arthur, the company's lawyer, was with him.

The secretaries hadn't arrived yet. It was obvious the mill wanted to keep the deal as quiet as possible until everything was settled. The door had been left open and we walked in the office behind them. Ubaldino's half brothers were stand-ing around Mr. Durham's oak desk and Mr. Arthur was handing out the copies of the deed to all of them. Everybody turned around in surprise to look at us, without realizing who we were. Only Doña Rosa stared at Ubaldino, and a slow, wide smile lit up her face.

'So it's you, Niño. It's so good to see you again,' she said. She got up from her chair and walked toward him, balancing her heavy body on a pair of high-heeled shoes she was obviously not used to wearing. She put her soft, moist hands on Ubaldino's face and kissed both his cheeks. The brothers began animatedly to embrace Ubaldino and to shake his hand. I could see my friend had begun to feel uncomfortable. His brothers' meek politeness, the unpretentious way they looked up and smiled at him all the time as though trying to prove something, made him feel guilty.

'How are things with you?' he said, giving each a small pat on the back. 'I can't believe it's been almost fifteen years since we saw each other last!' he added, looking at Doña Rosa.

He walked to the center of the room and shook hands with Mr. Durham and Mr. Arthur. They had already gotten over their amazement at seeing him there, and they pretended not to mind. They were as well acquainted as everyone else in Guamaní of the feud that had raged for years between the Fonts and the De la Valles, and they guessed Ubaldino's interest in the sale had something to do with it.

'We'll have to celebrate this little family reunion,' said Mr. Durham, offering everybody a chair. 'We don't have a rendezvous like this every day! It's worth at least a toast, so that it will appear tomorrow in Mr. Hermenegildo Martínez's news column in *The Nation*.' He took out a bottle of rum from the desk drawer and served everybody a drink. We all emptied our glasses, hoping that it wouldn't go to our heads on our still-breakfastless stomachs. Mr. Durham and Mr. Arthur looked silently at Ubaldino, who laughed sardonically and pushed his hat back from his forehead.

'I came to congratulate you. With the money from the sale of Diamond Dust you'll all be able to celebrate and move on to the capital.'

Mr. Durham shook his head in disappointment, as though he couldn't believe his eyes. 'Haven't you heard? Don Julio had some debts with the National City Bank and your brothers insist on paying them, instead of letting those little obligations rest in peace. We've already spoken to the bank, and they are more than willing to do so, but Doña Rosa won't listen.' Doña Rosa grew pale when she heard him. She leaned forward and looked abashed at the floor, shifting her weight on the chair.

'I am Don Julio Font's widow,' she said softly, 'and our first concern here today is to clear the dead man's name of slander. I don't know whether Niño Ubaldino has also come to sell his shares and set things to right, but I'm sure he agrees with us about his father.' Her voice was surprisingly steady, as if she really believed she had been Don Julio's wife and had a legal right to his name.

I suddenly noticed Ubaldino had gone pale; beads of perspiration stood out on his forehead. 'I haven't come here to sell,' he said, setting his glass down on the table. 'I've come to buy!' The sudden silence in the room made the hum of the ceiling fan sound like a power engine. I looked at Ubaldino in horror. If we hindered the sale of Diamond Dust there were sure to be reprisals against us, and our campaign would be at an end. I thought Ubaldino had gone out of his mind. He had let his pride get the better of him, because of his father's foolish amorous exploits.

'Buy Diamond Dust? And how do you propose to do so?' Mr. Arthur asked. 'You'd need thirty thousand dollars to better the option we've already signed with Doña Rosa and her sons.'

'He would need at least two hundred thousand,' corrected Mr. Durham, 'because that would be the price of the option, in case we decided to sell, which is not the case.'

Mr. Arthur had begun to take a pack of new bills out of his business case, and he set it down next to the copies of the deed, which were lying ready to be signed on the desk. 'There's some cash left for you in the briefcase, if you should decide to sell your five shares,' he told Ubaldino briskly. 'I suggest you sell them to us today, before the National City Bank forecloses a loan they made to your great-aunts and which they've been very lenient on. I heard they've been running late these past few months on the payments, and they might just lose their house in Guamaní.'

Ubaldino picked up the money and counted the bills one by one, making sure there was thirty thousand dollars in the pack. Then he put it back on the table and dug into his pockets with both hands, unceremoniously taking out a jumble of necklaces, bracelets, earrings, and rings that, as they were unwrapped and had been taken out of their cases, suddenly glittered with hallucinating brightness in the room. 'It seems to be almost poetic justice: Diamonds must come to diamonds and Dust to dust,' he joked as he disdainfully let the jewels fall one by one on top of the legal deeds. 'Mr. Arthur and Mr. Durham are going to have to do a little research work; they never should have set up this deal behind my back.'

Mr. Durham's face had gone from deep pink to purple. He threw a furious look at Mr. Arthur, but kept silent. 'It's not a matter of whether you want to sell me your option or not,' Ubaldino explained to them cordially. 'On our island, when the heirs of a business contract a sale without the knowledge or consent of a minority shareholder, such a shareholder has first right to acquire the whole property for the same price previously agreed on. In other words, my half brothers have no choice but to sell me Diamond Dust for the same thirty thousand dollars you had settled upon, and there's nothing you can do about it, because I don't owe the National City Bank a cent.' Ubaldino was right. The law he was referring to was known as the Right of Recall, and it was an ancient law of the Spanish Legal Codex that Mr. Arthur and Mr. Durham knew nothing about.

Ubaldino and I returned victorious to Guamaní that same afternoon, and we published the news of Diamond Dust's rescue on the front page of *The Nation*. As a result, there were fireworks, banquets, and parties thrown by our friends all over town, and a few months later Ubaldino was elected Union Party senator."

VII.

THE OATH

Titina showed me into Laura's bedroom and, after taking me to her bedside, disappeared from sight. A powerful smell of camphor assaulted my nostrils and I had to half close my eyes to get used to the dark. I saw the cathedral, the De la Valles' centuries-old caisson bed, famous throughout the district for its headboard made from an antique altarpiece, as well as for its brocaded purple canopy and feathered bedposts, which made it look like a horse-drawn catafalque. All the De la Valles had been born under its hallowed shade, and they boasted that its framework had been built from the revered remains of the ship in which Juan Ponce de León, their ancestor, had sailed to the island.

The vision of Laura laid out on the bed took my breath away, she was so beautiful. The embroidered coverlets in which she had been swaddled underlined the silhouette of a body still youthful in its ripeness. Wrapped around her neck, arms, and wrists glowed the fabled De la Valle gems, which I immediately recognized, having seen them once before many

63

years ago when Ubaldino had rescued Diamond Dust from
the ravenous grip of Snow White Sugar Mills. Laura opened
her eyes and looked at me. A strange tranquility emanated
from her profile, which made me think of a saint's relic
carved in soft ivory, blessing me with its quietude. In spite of
being partially drugged she smiled, as though defying the
pain that lay in wait for her, savagely crouched in the room's
brooding silence. She sighed deeply and turned her head
slowly on the pillow toward the right side of the bed, where
a screen door could be seen opening onto the terrace domi-
nating Diamond Dust's scrupulously cared for cane fields. It
had finally stopped raining, and through the languid pleats of
the curtains that rippled in the breeze I could see their
shining sheaves stirring their incredible green in the late-
afternoon sun.

Six times I've been asked the same question and six times
I've given the same answer (said Laura, when she finally
broke her silence) which lies buried in my heart like a handful of knives. Now I know how the Virgin of the Veronica
must have felt like when Christ had himself crucified for the
good of man, thus riveting her heart with silver blades. I'm
afraid that's the only answer I'll be able to give to the question you've probably come here to ask: why I decided to
bequeath all my worldly possessions to Gloria Camprubí and
her son. You'll never be able to understand the reason, Don
Hermenegildo, because in order to do so you'd have to be a
woman and you're a man, and men are always so painfully
unaware of the differences between us. I swear it's because
I'm a woman that you see me now lying here before you,
waiting patiently for death to arrive. Look at her sitting on
the chair next to my bed: she looks like an old friend watching over my sleep, tenderly nursing each breath I take. Death
is a woman, and for that reason she's courageous and just,
and never makes distinctions between mortals; she'll crush
the ignorant, the arrogant, and the wise alike under her icy
foot. Because I see myself in her, because I recognize myself
in her eyes, I really don't mind dying, Don Hermenegildo,
and in a few minutes I'll surrender myself gratefully unto her

arms. Death is the twin of love and mother of us all, she struggles equally for men and women and never accepts differences of caste or class. It's death that quickens us and brings us forth on sheets of love, clasped between sleep and wakefulness and barely breathing for a spell, and thus my death shall be like everybody else's death, as majestic and as pathetic as a king or a beggar's, neither more nor less. For that reason, although you may never truly understand my story, I'm going to try to tell it with my last breath.

After my passing there'll be no more De la Valles reigning over the emerald fields of Diamond Dust; none that shall be able to accumulate bags of gold in underground vaults; none that shall again sit at our dining-room table, strutting their false pride over its polished surface like well-fed peacocks and surrounded by the twelve leather shields that were once supposed to belong to Charlemagne's Knights and that were ridiculously made into chairs by Ubaldino's aunts; none that shall lie again under the Episcopal canopy of this bed which shelters my body from the cruel winds of passage, offering my shadow its sacred refuge during its last trial.

Laura became silent and I feared the effort she was making would exhaust her remaining strength, so that she wouldn't be able to go on speaking. Titina came into the room at that moment, carrying a cup of orange blossom tea that she set down on the night table, and Gloria walked in after her. I hadn't seen her for many years and she had aged considerably; she looked very different from when she used to attend the parties at Guamaní, triumphantly entering the elegant houses of those in the highest social circles arm in arm with Nicolás, but she seemed unaware of the change. All her movements, the way she walked swinging her hips and head held high, were still those of a woman sure of her beauty, exerting her sovereignty over the eyes of men. She was wearing an old-fashioned mauve-colored dress, with a steep neckline baring the abyss of her breasts; her hair rose on her shoulders like a cloud of gunpowder and a pair of mauve snakeskin shoes flashed gaudily under her skirt. She went by without so much as looking at me, as if I were a ghost and not really sitting there, and helped Titina prop Laura up on the bed, tenderly rearranging her feather pillows. They then began to slowly feed her the tea with a spoon. This done, they both sat down at the foot of the bed, as though waiting for Laura to wake up and continue telling her story.

The sick woman seemed to have fallen asleep and was silent for a long while. The gems that covered her body glittered faintly in the surrounding gloom, keeping time with the slow, almost evanescent rhythm of her breathing. I felt more and more distressed sitting there in the dark, exhausted by so much anguish and disillusionment. I wracked my brain trying to think what I could do to keep Arístides and his sisters from selling Diamond Dust, but couldn't come up with anything. I didn't dare ask about the will, and, in the chaos of opened drawers and upturned clothes of the dying woman's room, I wouldn't even have known where to begin to look. After listening to Arístides's shameful admissions, in any case, I wasn't sure it was worth trying to find. I felt loath to give him the help he had asked of me.

I began to get up from my chair to leave the room, but my weight must have made the wood creak indiscreetly because the sick woman suddenly came out of her langour. She looked up at me in surprise, as though the river of memory had suddenly tossed her up on the desolate vastness of the bed and left her there, defenseless and stranded, so that she hardly knew how she had arrived on its forsaken shores.

Ubaldino and I had a good life, Don Hermenegildo; for thirty years we were the happiest couple in Guamaní. This doesn't mean that we didn't have our little mishaps during our first years together, like for example when Doña Elvira and Doña Estefana found out about our impending marriage. From their standpoint, my last name wasn't patrician enough for a De la Valle, and they therefore proceeded to try to dissuade Ubaldino from marrying me. My father, Don Bon Bon Latoni, was a Corsican emigré whose father had made a small fortune in the coffee mountains of Utuado during the last half of the nineteenth century. I was born in those mountains, and grew to hate the difficult art of making the coffee trees grow. The Arabian coffee bean was the most highly appreciated by buyers in Europe, and Father spent his life planting those trees by the thousands, tenderly sheltering their childlike, delicate branches under the deep shades of yagrumo and moca trees, or behind humid, rustling banana bushes. When I grew up, I soon felt stifled by mountain life, where friends seldomly came to visit, and I begged my father to send me away to school.

In the coastal towns I discovered a marvelous new world, which had been kept hidden from me in the mountains. I saw that everything I had been told since childhood about the northerners who had arrived on the island a few years before was a shameful lie. If on the range we had to ride a mule train for hours to get to the family plantation house, because the roads were winding over crevices where even the goats had to eat with emergency brakes on, on the plains the northerners had built wide, well-planned roads that one could traverse comfortably in gaily painted automobiles and buses; if on the mountains there was no way to cross the soul-shaking rapids that rushed over dolphin-blue boulders at the bottom of the riverbeds, the northerners had built steel bridges that flew over them and spanned them like delicate silver spider webs; if before the northerners arrived there were only a handful of public schools on the island, there were seven hundred schools and thirty thousand children enrolled a year after their arrival, and the problem of our eight hundred thousand illiterate souls began to be resolved; the towns on the plain became scattered with ample, graceful buildings, schools and hospitals with whitewashed columns and wide pink verandahs that housed the ignorant and the sick.

The foreigners were dynamos, men of unflagging action; they were all young and handsome, engineers, architects, doctors, energetic entrepreneurs who believed they could transform the world and bring us the blessings of progress. They were brimming with idealism: they didn't *have* to civilize the world, they themselves were perfectly happy in their own land, where they had built marvelous cities and practically wiped out poverty, and yet they believed it their duty to better the destiny of others. And so they came to this ancient isle in the middle of the Caribbean, a primitive, cannibal sea, to give a generous helping hand to those so long forsaken by the Spanish God. It's true that they brought the island's bourgeoisie to its knees, but as political and civil leaders they were a no-good lot to begin with, full of false pride and patriotic feelings when it came to singing the glories of their emerald reefs pinned on the sapphire breast of the sea, but lazily ignorant of those scientific and technological advances of agriculture and industry with which they could truly help their country, and utterly devoid of compassion for their fellow human beings. Because the truth is, Don Hermenegildo, that when the northerners landed here, Guamaní's sugar plantations were hell on earth. The methods of planting and reaping were so primitive, under a sky that simmered like a cauldron of live coals over one's head, that the only way for the field hands to survive the heat and the hunger was by carrying small flasks of rum slung from their necks, so that they could take a swig every time they felt the earth sink under their feet. Although slavery had been abolished, they were obliged to cut at least four hundred kilos of sugarcane a day, their meager wages could only be taken on credit at the company store, and they were whipped for the least infraction of company rules. In other words, the souls of thousands of field hands were wafted away to the sky by those selfsame proud, blue smokestacks, which you have so romantically described in your novels about Guamaní's haut monde.

All this was done away with when the foreigners came: they established modern methods of reaping and planting; the field hands were treated like human beings instead of like slaves; their children could go to school; they were given adequate housing and shoes. In other words, the foreigners were a blessing to the poor and to the middle class as well, albeit a scourge to the rich. They brought us glass panes for our windows to keep out the rain and penicillin to fend off malaria; they brought us the telephone, the telegraph, and the cable; they brought us electricity, running water, and the safety pin to boot; and for the first time in memory a photographer, Walter B. Townsend, who had come over in Admiral

Sampson's fleet, walked freely the streets of Guamaní. Dressed
in safari jacket, knee-high cordovan boots, and wide-brimmed
felt hat to fend off the snakes and the poisonous seeds that
might drop from the trees, he gave testimony to the world of
our immemorial squalor, of our palm-thatched huts and our
miserable mud streets, where stray dogs went so hungry they
would attack women and children in packs, where children
walked about barefoot and naked, floating about like tiny
balloons on spindly legs, with bloated, parasitic abdomens
sticking out before them. These well-known sights of my youth
left a lasting imprint on my memory, Don Hermenegildo,
and for this reason I hold the foreigners in high esteem.
Many years later I couldn't have been more pleased when
three of my daughters married these civilized men.

When I first came to this house as a newlywed, I realized
the family I had married into was a strange one indeed. Doña
Elvira and Doña Estefana were always very conscious of
what they called the privileges of their caste. They would
have preferred a Cáceres or an Acuña, with a coat of arms
sparkling on her little finger, but they had to make do with
plain Laura Latoni as consort for their prince. When Father
died and left me a small inheritance, the red gold that bloomed
on our coffee trees became a powerful persuasion, and soon
the vulgar jingle of my last name acquired an attractive ring.
Ubaldino, once he had successfully managed to wrestle the
hacienda and the house he had been born in from the owners
of Snow White, moved to live here with his great-aunts. He
had already been living in the house for a few years when he
met me, and during that time had gone out of his way to
modernize it and make it livable. It evidently had a very
special meaning for all of them, and I immediately noticed
that the aunts lived obsessed with keeping it in perfect order.
The family furniture, china, and silver, which had been here
from their childhood days, was still intact, as Don Julio
and Doña Rosa had taken very good care of things. The
family coat of arms, three dogs hounding a fox up a tree,
hung in every sitting room as well as in the study, and
Ubaldino had had it embroidered on his underwear, painted
on the Limoges dinner plates, enameled on the Venetian

glassware, engraved on the silver serving dishes and even on the personal gold chamber pot he had inherited from his grandparents. He had also hung portraits of all his ancestors, except his father, of whom I never saw a picture or a photograph in the house, in the formal living room, so that the parlor resembled a gathering of stiff, tuxedo-clad ghosts, sitting up to all hours of the night and talking gibberish to one another about the glories of Diamond Dust.

The aunts, on the other hand, would spend days on end poring over a set of heavy parchment tomes bound in soddy, grimy goatskin, tracing the De la Valles' complicated family tree. With breathless amazement they would then proclaim to the world that such and such's grandmother was the daughter of Countess Tosspot, or that such and such's grandfather was the Marquis of Merdeland, grandson of the Duke of Feculence, and for that reason the De la Valles were direct descendants of the daughters of El Cid. In spite of their living on a tight income (the mill, which Ubaldino had just bought from the northerners, was still just breaking even and the aunts had to earn their living giving piano lessons and embroidering lace shawls), the family's delirium of greatness made them unable to live without servants. Titina and Néstor's services were not enough for them, and the aunts had painted a veritable army of turbaned, liveried valets on the swinging doors of the dining and living rooms, so as to create the illusion of being served coralline lobsters boiled alive, or amber rice with wild partridge hens from silver trays.

This pompous megalomania used to drive me out of my mind at first, but I finally learned to ignore it. What I couldn't bear, though, was listening to the old women's constant prattle about which families of Guamaní had a strain of black blood in them, and which had managed to remain white. One day I couldn't stand their ugly habit any longer, and asked them sarcastically if they didn't think they were really pushing the point, since in recent years there had been such a great number of intermarriages in Guamaní's haut monde that by now everybody was related and probably not a single family could be considered white. They looked at me in horror, taken aback by my remark, and I couldn't help but burst out laughing. That evening, however, as we were lying in bed under this lace canopy, I let Ubaldino know what I really thought. " 'If your aunts believe they're so much better than the rest of the world, Guamaní included, that they mistake their shit for gold droppings and their urine for Santa Rosa de Lima's perfumed pee, I won't contradict their wisdom. But please ask them not repeat their half-witted jokes about who is black and who is white in front of me, or they'll simply have to go live someplace else.' "

Ubaldino knew very well I could carry out my threat. I had just put all the money from the sale of my father's coffee plantation into Diamond Dust, and I had done so as a private investor, since I had only consented on our marriage after having signed a separation agreement of all our worldly goods. I had thus become proprietor of half the mill, and my marriage had become a successful combination of business and love. The years went by and Ubaldino proved to be a perfect husband, always eager to please me. We always had a good stew boiling over our pot, and therefore had no trouble coddling each other's tastes. When he was elected senator he became very busy, so that I was forced to take over a great deal of the management of the mill. After a while, thanks to our joint efforts we were able to turn Diamond Dust into one of the most productive businesses in Guamaní, second only to Snow White's monster mill. A few years later Ubaldino's aunts died, embalmed in the powdered gold breathed forth by dubious ancestral tomes; our children were born, grew up, and went to school; and we all lived in harmony and peace.

Only one dark cloud hung on our perfect sky. In spite of the fact that our daughters were undoubtedly a good catch, and that they were not only beautiful but born to fame and fortune under the De la Valle name, they were never invited to the parties that were given at the homes of the well-to-do in Guamaní. As I wasn't born in town myself, I was unable to help them. I'd always shunned the company of the sugar landowning families; they never could rise above the fact of having lost their political clout on the island, and had become a race of small, resentful men, ready to plunge the knife of rancor into their best friend's backs. At first my daughters waited patiently for the invitations to come, but after a while they became desperate.

It was at these family parties that girls of marriageable age were supposed to meet the young men who were to be their suitors, and not to be invited to them practically meant being sentenced to spinsterhood. It was then that, over Ubaldino's stubborn resistance, they began to accept the invitations of the families of Snow White Sugar and to attend their parties, crossing over the well-guarded frontiers of the mill to play tennis and to swim in their pool. They soon stopped going to mass every morning, eating rice and beans, Mont Blanc meringues, baba au rums, and other unhealthy foods that made them heavy and cowlike, and blossomed into spirited girls who were able to think for themselves. When they fell in love with the handsome blond gods who lived behind the silver cyclone fences of the company town, Ubaldino and I never really saw it as a family problem. When the time came, we would pass on Diamond Dust to Nicolás, who after all was destined by the Spanish tradition of *mayorazgo* to be the sole owner, and the rum distillery to Arístides, because he was second in line. The girls would all be given valuable lands, although not those pertaining to the mill itself, and thus would be adequately compensated for having been excluded from the mill.

Ubaldino and I had already begun to complete all the above arrangements for a peaceful retirement, as befits the conclusion of a well-balanced life, when I made a frightful discovery, Don Hermenegildo. During his political sojourns at the capital Ubaldino had contracted syphilis, and I was terrified of becoming infected; I had nightmares that my spinal cord would disintegrate, or that my body would break out in pustules, and I refused to have marital relations with him. Arístides had brought Gloria to our house as a nurse at that time, to help me take care of Ubaldino and to keep me company. Gloria comes from a family of modest means and therefore has a good head on her shoulders. She thinks the society fops of Guamaní are hilarious, always dressed in sugar-white linen suits and flaunting their handkerchiefs doused in Eau Imperial before the practical, navy-blue-suited businessmen from the north, in the hope of dazing them, so they'd let go their stranglehold. For this reason we soon became good friends. On day, two months after she began to work for us, we were sitting together on the balcony when she made a curious remark. She couldn't understand why everyone in the house spoke of Don Julio Font as if he had been a Spanish merchant, because when she was young she had heard a lot about him, and she was sure he didn't speak with a foreign accent.

I was astounded at her disclosure. When I asked her for more details about Don Julio she told me she knew quite a bit about him because she had been brought up in a hacienda on the other side of the valley, which today is almost a suburb of Guamaní, where Doña Rosa's sons, Ubaldino's half brothers, had settled down to work after they had been forced to leave this very same house. (This must have been at the same time Ubaldino took over Diamond Dust, and moved in here with his aunts.) There she had become a friend of their children, and had gotten to know Don Julio's illegitimate family rather well. I asked her if it was true that, as family lore would have it and as Aunt Emilia and Aunt Estefana used to tell everyone in Guamaní, Don Julio was a dangerously handsome man, with skin white as milk and cruel golden eyes speckled with green, and if he truly had that conquistador's proud, stalwart build, with bulwark arms and fortress-wide shoulders, which had so turned poor Doña Elvira's head when she fell head over heels in love with him. Gloria had been working on her embroidery, and she suddenly held her needle motionless in the air as she looked at me in surprise. For a moment she believed I was joking.

" 'I never met Don Julio, since he'd been dead several years before his family moved to my neighborhood, but they did say he was very good looking,' " she said, laughing. " 'However, from what I've heard, he didn't look at all like what you say. He was probably like his sons, dark-skinned, tall, and brawny; he was famous for being the most imposing horse tamer in the district.' "

A lightning bolt from heaven wouldn't have shaken me

more if it had split at my feet. I was dumbstruck with surprise, and had to make an effort to recover my self-control. So that had been the secret, the unmentionable mystery that had made the aunts send their niece to live in the country when she married Don Julio, away from the prying eyes of Guamaní's society: the refined Doña Elvira, educated in Paris amid silk cushions, had married a black man! That was the reason I could never find a single portrait, daguerreotype, or photograph of poor Don Julio Font in the house, while there were plenty of Doña Elvira, as well as of other De la Valle ancestors! That was why, when I guilelessly mentioned Don Julio's name in the elegant teas of Guamaní, silver teaspoons would drop unexpectedly on porcelain saucers, mowed down by mistrusting surprise, and the eyebrows of all the women present would rise like delicate whips of reproach over their eyes. That was the explanation why our poor daughters had always been snubbed in Guamaní's parties, because they had forbidden their cavalier sons to dance with them, and had warned them not to fall in love with quarteroons.

I can see by the pained expression on your face that this story is nothing new to you, Don Hermenegildo, that you are resigned to the fact that the De la Valles' secret is by now of public domain. As a close friend of Ubaldino you'll probably hate me for mentioning it, for spelling out in all the letters of that alphabet that death will soon root out from my tongue the fact that his father, Don Julio Font, was a black man. But such is, after all, the role of death: she evens us out at the last, and forces us to admit that we are all born equal, innocent of race and caste. In this country the splendors of nobility and purity of lineage are no more than a fool's frippery, roisterings from a jester's cap. The only lineage worth being proud of in this town is money; greenbacks are the only family tree that still stands in Guamaní. And while our false criollo aristocrats powder themselves with the sugar of respectability, as our family does with Diamond Dust, their fortunes keep running out between their fingers like sand and end up in Snow White's coffers.

I know this is a delicate point with you, especially since

you have set out to write the saga of Ubaldino's life, one of our island's most beloved caudillos, who may have been a barbarian but who was undoubtedly a patriot, as well, because he drew the innermost impulse of his being from the magical powers of the land from which he had inherited his family name. He had the sweetness and warmth of its soft, sabled topsoil, and he planted and reaped some of the lushest canes in the world; he had its fertile energy, as can be seen by the many illegitimate children he left behind; but for that very same reason he could never be ruthless like the businessmen of Snow White. Like most of our political leaders he, too, was an offspring of the Easter lamb that Queen Isabella the First of Spain had prophetically bequeathed us on our national coat of arms, and for that reason all he could do was defend his native lair as well as he could. He was never a monster of authority, a true Latin American caudillo as perhaps you would have written in your novel, Don Hermenegildo, or as Arístides certainly would have liked you to write. In a way this was to be expected, as a true caudillo will always be a projection of the land he lives in, and our island, as José Gautier Benítez sang in his poem long ago, has always been peace-loving, feminine, and childlike: *"Todo en tí es voluptuoso y leve,/dulce, apacible, halagador y tierno,/y tu mundo moral su encanto debe al dulce influjo de tu mundo externo."** And in any case there's so little of it to be proud of; our island is so small that when the northerners landed in the south, no sooner had they begun their march up the mountains than they were already getting their feet wet on the other side.

I have thought long and hard about all these things, Don Hermenegildo, and it's only at death's throes that I've begun to understand them. I foresee a time when all this rivalry and struggle for our fertile valley between the local landowners and northern investors will be but a legend whispered by the

---

*José Gautier Benítez, the romantic poet par excellence of Puerto Rican letters, was born in 1851 and died of tuberculosis in 1880 at the age of thirty. He is the author of "Canto a Puerto Rico," a poem in which for the first time the island's landscape is described. Gautier was also a combative and courageous journalist who fought for the island's independence from Spanish colonial rule. Gautier studied in a military academy in Spain, and his family belonged to the landed class of its time.

wind, a picturesque romance of the past. Because it's not our land but our port, the beautiful, shimmering bay of Guamaní, that will one day make our fortunes, as the land becomes less and less important to all of us. It's our island's destiny to become the gate to South as well as to North America, so that on our doorsill both continents will one day peacefully merge into one. And it's for this reason that I'm set on leaving Diamond Dust to Gloria and Nicolasito, because they are the children of that port, their unbribable tribal offspring. From the very first day of Gloria's arrival at our house, I was very much aware of her constant visits to the waterfront canteens and bars, where she soon became a sort of legendary prostitute, offering herself to all those ruined farmers who were about to emigrate to Chicago and New York, as well as to the new entrepreneurs who came from the north, and thus Nicolasito can be said to be the child of all. In her body, or if you prefer in her cunt, both races, both languages, English and Spanish, grew into one soul, into one wordweed of love. She's the priestess of our harbor; pythia of our island's future; of a time when a scanty, meager land that for centuries had condemned us to immobility and backwardness will ultimately have no importance and where our souls, our very lives will be determined by transformation and daring, in other words, by change. Our spirits will then be made quick-silver, and we will become the sailors of time's passage, the wizards of metamorphosis. If in ancient times our island was Spain's outpost for the discoveries of the New World, the magical frontier between the Tainos, the Caribs, and the Spanish conquistadors, in modern times it will become, as in *Midsummer Night's Dream*, a talking wall, or at least a chink in the wall. Through a chink in our tropical moss the North will talk to the South and the South will talk to the North, and one day they'll finally understand each other. And so I have instructed Gloria to sell our land progressively, piece by piece, to aid those who have already begun to emigrate to the mainland by the thousands, fleeing from the hell of the sugar plantation, to lend the honest effort of their arms and legs to other harvests more generously repaid; as well as to those who will undoubtedly return, perhaps after spending half their lives reaping California grapes, or driving a taxi through the cement jungle of New York, but with enough money in their pockets to buy a piece of their lost paradise back.

But I must come back to my story, Don Hermenegildo, to the story of the De la Valles' erring pride and of my own misfortune. When I belatedly discovered the De la Valles' secret I went through a difficult trial, which made me reassess the true purpose of my life. Not only was I repulsed by what it had revealed to me about Guamaní's haut monde; I was also angry, bereaved by the fact that I had learned of it at such a late date, when Ubaldino was already sick and it was impossible for me to face him with the truth as I would have wished. I realized then that Ubaldino had never really believed that ridiculous story of Doña Elvira's having been unwittingly murdered by Don Julio, supposedly a Spanish merchant, which his aunts had probably made up to save face with their friends. Don Julio had been born on the island of very dubious social origins, and Ubaldino had probably known the truth all along. It had been his desperate need to conceal this, not only before the beveled mirrors of Guamaní's casino but before the shaving mirror of his own *nécessaire*, that had led him to pretend a purity of blood he didn't possess.

Ubaldino was growing rapidly worse. During the day he'd run naked out of his bedroom, and soon it was necessary to lock him up in it, but his obscene oaths could still be heard echoing through the house. He screamed and swore, cursing me for being his jailer and threatening to kill me. Arístides and my daughters refused to enter their father's room, so that I had to rely entirely on Gloria and Titina to help me carry a cross that was becoming heavier to bear every day. At that time I noticed Gloria's presence had a balsamic effect on Ubaldino. If either Titina or I brought him his food he'd go into a paroxysm of rage, but if Gloria went near him he immediately became quiet, and would eat from her hand like a child. Seeing the sick man's positive response, we soon arrived at a tacit understanding: Gloria would do everything in her power to get Ubaldino to fall in love with her, so that in his insane state he would pin his hopes on a deceptive mirage which would tame his fury, as long as I would remember her in my will.

It was relatively easy to carry out our plan: old people feed more on what they can whiff than on what they can chew, and Ubaldino's illness had already ravaged his body to such a degree that his dream of Gloria's love was more than enough for him to be happy. And thus he lived peacefully the last months of his life, lulled by the odor of fresh bread that never quite finished baking at her oven's door. His dream kept him alive: he'd watch out for Gloria's comings and goings through the house as she performed her nursing chores, and forgot all about me at night as well as at noontime when he took his nap. I felt I was saved: soon I was able to move to a separate room where I could sleep peacefully by myself.

Everything was going fine, and I was already thanking the Almighty for my good fortune at having been able to rid myself so easily of canker and its ulcers, when Arístides had to spoil it all. He had been the one to bring Gloria to us in the first place, having given her a job when she was a struggling girl fresh out of nursing school; and this made him believe he had special rights over her body and soul. As she was my personal companion and friend, I would have liked to sit her with us at dinnertime, as well as to include her in our family's social gatherings, but Arístides was dead against it from the start, claiming that she was a mulatto and that it was unseemly for us to be intimate with improper gentry.

I'll never live down the shame I felt at the time at my son's behavior, Don Hermenegildo. May death, sitting at my right hand, be witness to the suffering I went through. And I didn't just suffer for myself, fearful as I was of Gloria's becoming annoyed by Arístides's uncouth behavior and of her quitting her job, leaving me without a shield to fend off venereal disease, but I was also upset for Gloria's sake, because she's a woman like me and I consider her my friend. Arístides slighted her at every turn; he made her help in the kitchen, as well as with the laundry and ironing, chores that traditionally belonged only to Titina; and whenever she entered a room he'd get up and leave, furiously slamming the door.

Fortunately things began to change for the better when Nicolás returned from France. Nicolás was always my favorite child, not because he was the eldest, as Arístides cynically insists, but because he'd always been the most generous and compassionate. A short time after he came back, I explained Gloria's difficult situation, how she had to stand Arístides's constant abuse, and he immediately offered to help me. He thought about it for a while and eventually came up with an answer: he could marry Gloria, so she'd have nothing more to fear from Arístides and wouldn't quit her job.

I thought the heavens had finally pitied me, Don Hermenegildo, but on this island when it rains it pours, and things never turn out the way you want them to. In this Vale of Tears man will propose, but God will dispose, and it's not wise to kick against the goad, because you'll only lame yourself. The wedding arrangements were settled in absolute privacy; Gloria, to my great relief, agreed to everything from the start. After Ubaldino's death her marriage to Nicolás would be annulled, and the services she had rendered the family would be generously repaid.

You know the rest of the story well, Don Hermenegildo. Nicolás died six months after the wedding. When I heard the news of the accident I didn't shed a tear. I opened the door myself when the funeral wake arrived at the house, after a week-long search for the boy's remains in the woods. Arístides helped carry in the casket, together with the acolytes and the priest, and I remember they were all perspiring as it went in the door. Once they set it down in the living room, which was full of family and friends, I threw myself sobbing on the lid, clamoring to see what was left of my son one last time. Arístides and my daughters held me back.

" 'Thank God He took him away from us, Mother, they said in a loud voice for all to hear. This way no De la Valle will ever marry a black woman again.' "

The absurdity of their words hit me like a slap on the cheek, Don Hermenegildo, and at first I didn't know whether to laugh or cry. I kneeled before the coffin and did both. I remember that when I finally came to I was holding on desperately to the casket, as though Nicolás had just been taken away from me. And then I screamed at the top of my voice, so that all Guamaní might hear me, what was it that made the De la Valles believe they were better than Gloria or the rest of the world, when Don Julio Font, their grandfather, had been a black man; swearing at the top of my lungs that, in return for their inane pride and because the De la Valles' name was a farce and no one in that house really had any right to use it, when I died I'd disinherit all of them and leave my shares of Diamond Dust to Gloria Camprubí and her son.

Laura's voice had become increasingly weaker as she talked, so that at the end it was no more than a whisper which faded into the shadows of the room. I knew she had stopped breathing because her jewels no longer glimmered in the dark, settling over her body like an icy constellation of stars. Titina, on the other side of the bed, had begun to pray, her face a paroxysm of tears. And then I saw Gloria walk out of a dark corner and resolutely cross the room. She came near the bed, and before I could do anything to prevent it, she shut Laura's eyes with her fire-red polished fingernails. She didn't say a word or even look at me. She slid her hand brazenly under the lace pillowcases and took out Laura's will from under them. Then she slowly, deliberately tore it in half and threw it into the wastepaper basket, before walking out of the room without looking back.

VIII.

HOMAGE TO MOREL CAMPOS*

I KNEW IT, TITINA, I TOLD YOU SO A HUNDRED TIMES, HOW
stupid of you to believe in them, to insist on being faithful
to the family, trusting Niño Ubaldino to leave Néstor and
you the zinc-roofed cabin at the end of the garden in his will,
may God shelter him in his bosom like a martyr as the fire
begins to consume the foundations of this house. You should
never have visited Don Hermenegildo in his office, you fool,
you should never have gone to fetch him thinking he'd come

---

*Juan Morel Campos was born in Ponce, a coastal town on the south of the island, in 1857,
and died in 1896. He was a disciple of Manuel Tavarez and later became the sole brass tuba
in the military band "The Batallion of Hunters of Madrid," where he learned instrumenta-
tion and how to be an orchestra conductor. Upon finishing his military duty, he formed his
own dance orchestra, and soon his compositions made him famous. Morel transformed the
simple "habanera" into a ballroom dance, separating it from its humble origins by giving it
an extraordinary rhythmic and harmonic sophistication. Among his most famous dances are
"Maltido Amor," "Laura y Georgina," "Ten Piedad," "Mis Penas," "Alma Sublime,"
"Vano Empeno," "Felices Dias," and "No Me Toques." Moral Campos, who was black and
humble of origin, was to a great extent self-taught. He was the first Puerto Rican composer
to utilize the negroid element in his compositions, as for example in the complex rhythms of
"marumba" and "guaracha," which he inserts in the musical trios "La Majabaca" and "La
Conga."

and help us, trusting him to defend us from that pack of vultures, when the De la Valles and their friends are all birds of a feather.

If Don Hermenegildo came to the house, if he agreed to leave his elegant, leather-upholstered solicitor's office where he's locked himself up for years writing a sentimental romance about Don Ubaldino, he certainly didn't intend to help us, or to hand us Diamond Dust on a silver platter, but rather to let Arístides and his sisters know about Doña Laura's secret will. Although in a way I'm not sorry he came, and I'm glad you invited him to do so, because now Don Hermenegildo will never be able to finish his novel. He's probably still sitting next to the dead woman, staring into the dark and inventing new lies, new ways of twisting around the story he heard from the lips of the protagonists of this tasteless melodrama. And if he should get away, if he should somehow manage to escape from the river of blue benzine that we poured a minute ago over the mounds of dry cane stalks carelessly left piled up around the houses of sugarcane haciendas; if he should succeed in jumping out the window, for example, from the third floor to the garden below, which is swirling this very minute with lighted cinders like a subsidiary of hell, we'll still have the satisfaction of knowing that nobody will believe his tale about the man he maintained was a leader and a statesman, and who had been corrupt for so long. Facts have a strange way of facing down fiction, Titina, and if Don Hermenegildo's aborted novel was to have been a series of stories that contradicted one another like a row of falling dominoes, our story, the one we've taken the authority to write, will eradicate them all, because it will be the only one in which word and deed will finally be loyal to each other, in which a true correspondence between them will finally be established.

Stop crying, Titina, you mustn't cry any more for Doña Elvira, for Nicolás or for Doña Laura. From now on you must sing my favorite song, that tacky, sentimental *danza* by Morel Campos that Nicolás and I used to sing as we made love long ago in these same cellars which you and I are lighting up now. Listen to the cane stalks bursting around us like kindling, empty and dry like the gibberish of Don Hermenegildo's novel; rejoice with me because Diamond Dust will finally go up in smoke. When I listened to Doña Laura's story a few minutes ago I finally realized what we had to do, Titina; what this land, spent from the struggle that had gone on for so long in its bosom, was ordering us to do. You know Doña Laura's story better than I do, how many times she was betrayed by her husband. And it wasn't just his sordid love affairs that made her suffer, but his just as sordid political affairs, which had rent her family asunder for decades. Doña Laura gave her husband's campaigns her total support, because she believed he really did want to do the best for his country. But Don Ubaldino betrayed her, and once he became senator he quickly forgot his patriotic ideals. He became just another politician, who could recite poems by heart about the tragic condition of a country that could now effectively rivet its heart to the whirling wheels of progress, but that had lost the sense of its own time; a country where history now began in 1898, when the northerners arrived on the island, and everything before that had never taken place; a country that had had to sacrifice the language it had thought and loved in for centuries for the language of electricity, of modern sanitary facilities, of intelligently built roads and bridges—in short, of survival. But he never did anything about it. He soon realized how difficult it was to juggle from left to right, and that he couldn't keep up the way of life his senatorial appointment had made possible, the European cruises, the *paso fino* horses, the mistresses and the Rolls-Royces without giving his support to corrupt politicians, and thus every morning, as he shaved and did his twenty minutes of weightlifting, he'd practice a series of forgetting exercises, to weaken his memory as much as possible, and opposed the advanced social legislation proposed by the northerners at every opportunity. He thus fought fiercely against the northerners' efforts to democratize the town, against the right to strike, the minimum wage, and the eight-hour work day, striving to keep Guamaní's inhabitants in the same state of abject poverty they had known for centuries.

When Doña Laura decided that Nicolasito and I should

one day inherit her part of Diamond Dust, at first I thought
she had gone out of her mind, that the loneliness to which
her children had abandoned her had finally broken her stam-
ina. Nicolás would have done anything for his mother, and
she treated me like her own daughter. This is why Nicolás
and I were married, to please her, because marriage really
wasn't important to us; she knew that married or not we'd
always be together, be it in the heights of heaven or the
depths of hell, where Guamaní society would readily have
thrown us. It was all the same to us, so powerful was the love
that consumed us. With the years I had grown to love Doña
Laura and I forgave her her miserliness, because she was so
alone and so afraid of death. This is why I never left the
house after Nicolás's accident, although I felt tempted to do
so that very day. I loved her for the memories we shared and
because I could conjure up Nicolás's presence more easily,
when she called out to his ghost from the balconies of the
house. At her side I felt nearer to him, as though together we
could warm the sad mementos of his bones. And it was
because we both lived for memory, while Don Ubaldino, as
well as Arístides and his sisters, lived for forgetfulness, that I
began to think that perhaps it was morally right that Nicolasito
and I should inherit Diamond Dust.

Nicolás loved the valley of Guamaní and its people, and it
was because of them that he lost his life. You must never
forget that, Titina, sear it on your memory with this fire-
brand I hold next to the ausubo beams of this same stinking
servant's room where you and I rested so many nights, after
having worked all day for our keep. Nicolás was also aware
that memory was very important, and he knew that Guamaní
had never been a paradise, as Don Hermenegildo says in his
romantic novel, but that for centuries it had been an epidemic-
infested hole, where most of the Guamaneños remained illiterate and before turning thirty-five would die by the hundreds
from tuberculosis, uncinariasis, and hunger. He knew the
local hacienda owners were to blame for this, long before the
arrival of the northerners on the island; and his father was a
typical example of it. This is why, only a month after being
named president of the mill, he began to distribute land

among the peasants, offering them the opportunity to build
their own houses and paying them a decent salary, measures
that infuriated Arístides and drove Don Ubaldino insane
with anger, cursing his son because of it more than once.

Doña Laura never discovered the truth about Nicolás's
accident, and after all was said and done, it finally didn't
matter. Both his father and his brother hated him, so that
what the right hand would hesitate to do the left did willingly, taking care to turn the other way. Once Nicolás was
buried Doña Laura ordered an investigation. A brigade of
private detectives combed the site of the accident and picked
up one by one the remains of the wreck, of motor and
fuselage. There was evidence enough to establish sabotage,
but no proof as to the culprits. When Doña Laura learned of
this, she decided to leave Diamond Dust to Nicolasito and
myself.

So you see, Titina, you really shouldn't have gone to fetch
Don Heremenegildo and have him come here, you idiot; you
and your doomed love for Niño Ubaldino and his children,
for the hacienda house with its balconies opening onto a sea
of cane. You must understand that everything he wrote about
us was a lie, and that the only thing that will remain of his
novel will be the allegiance between fire and words. Don't
cry any more, you foolish woman, don't you see none of it
matters any more, that Arístides and his sisters would never
have let you keep the bungalow Niño Ubaldino had left you
in his will. The important thing is we still have each other, so
that now we can sing together the words of that old song, as
we light up the cellar of the house with our torches:

> Your love is a bird which has found its voice
> Your love has finally nested in my heart;
> Now I know why it burns
> When I remember you.

II.
THE GIFT

No one expected Merceditas Cáceres, on the day Carlotta Rodriguez was expelled from the Sacred Heart, to hang her silk sash from the doorknob, drop her medal of the Congregation of the Angels in the alms box, and walk out through the school's portico arm in arm with her friend, head held high and without deigning once to look back, with that gesture of paramount disdain so commonplace in those of her social class. Next to her through the half-light of the entrance hallway went Carlotta, her huge body gently swaying forward like a tame heifer's, her thick mask of makeup running down her cheeks in furrows, hopelessly staining her white blouse and the starched collar of her uniform with its varicolored tears.

At that moment Merceditas was giving up, in the name of friendship, ten, perhaps twenty crowns of roses that already shimmered like snowy rings at the bottom of the wardrobe where the nuns kept the prizes to be awarded on graduation day, while Carlotta went in pursuit of hers, that astonishing

89

fan of golden peacock's feathers that was very soon to gird her forehead like a crown. There at the school's hallway she left behind, amid the rustling of blue pleated skirts and starched white shirts, the many honors she had so arduously worked for during her three and a half years at the academy, the ribbons and medals that now would never shine on her breast, while Carlotta went in quest of hers, of the bottles of cheap perfume and of the flowered handkerchiefs, of the earrings and bangles in gift boxes of garish velvet, which were to be so lovingly presented to her by the members of her retinue on her coronation day. Followed by her silver parade floats, she would walk a few days later down Ponce de León Avenue (as she would also do months later down the principal thoroughfares of Rio de Janeiro, New Orleans, and even Surinam), outfitted in her eighteen-karat gold robe and revealing, on the diamond-studded brim of her décolletage, her enormous dark breasts, sustained by a vision of the world that deserved, in the judgment of the venerable ladies of the Sacred Heart, the steaming torments of the cauldrons of hell.

The mango had been a present from Carlotta, who had brought it secretly into the school after spending the weekend at her father's house. She took it out of her pocket at recess and held it before her friend, balancing it in the palm of her hand.

"It was a present from the members of the carnival's committee at lunch today," she said, smiling. "It's of a variety called Columbus's kidney; sweet like a sugar loaf and soft like butter. Keep it; it's my gift to you."

Merceditas accepted the mango with a laugh and they walked together toward the small grove of honeyberries that grew at the end of the school's patio. It was their favorite haunt, because the shade of the trees provided a temporary release from the heat and also because the nuns rarely patrolled that part of the garden. Carlotte was describing the details of the lunch to her, all of which had had to do with the carnival's theme.

"Silver candelabra and plenas, cod fritters and Venetian tablecloths. You would have enjoyed the combination if you'd been there to see it. But what I really liked best was that the

committee should have thought of that beautiful mango, Columbus's kidney, as an official gift. In the past, carnival
queens were always presented with a jewel, be it a gold ring
or a bracelet, on the day of their appointment."

Merceditas laughed again loudly, her head thrown back,
thinking her friend was teasing her.

"It's called like that not in memory of Christopher Columbus's kidney, though, but of Juan Ponce de León's," Carlotta added. "He brought that variety of mango over from
India, from a city called Columbus, and planted it himself on
the island."

Merceditas looked at her friend and saw that, in spite of
the historical blunder she had just made, she was speaking in
earnest. "Then it's settled? You've accepted the appointment
of carnival queen?" she asked.

"I'll be the first truly Creole queen in Santa Cruz, don't
you think?" she said, rubbing her hand lightly over her dark
cheeks. "Before queens were always so pale and insipid. If
Don Juan Ponce de León should have seen me he would have
picked me. Spaniards always preferred swarthy girls."

Merceditas tried her best to imagine her friend decked out
in silk ruff, crown, and farthingale, but to no avail. Carlotta
was too plump, and she lacked all the necessary social graces.
It was precisely because of that, and because of her merry,
candid disposition, that she had picked her as her friend.

"It's just that I can't picture you dressed up like a
queen."

Carlotta smiled reassuringly and put her hand affectionately on her friend's shoulder. "Cleopatra was plump and
rowdy, and you have to admit, from the pictures of her we've
seen in the *Treasure of Youth*, that she never had hair as nice as
mine."

Merceditas looked at her from the corner of her eye. It was
true; her friend had a beautiful mane of hair that she had
always admired, and which she wore carefully combed in heavy
mahogany tresses, in compliance to the school's regulations.
"Many visitors will come to town for the feasts," Carlotta
added enthusiastically, "and if in the past we were famous for
our tobacco and our coffee, in the future we'll be known

everywhere for our carnival." They walked on together in silence, until they got to the wire fence that marked the end of the school's property at the edge of the garden. On the other side of the fence they could see the Portugués's stony riverbed, glinting in the sun like an unpaved highway.

"Aren't you afraid Mother Artigas may not like the idea of your carnival having to do with Juan Ponce de León? You know how finicky she is about historical matters."

"Whoever wants the sky must learn to fly," Carlotta answered, shrugging her shoulders. "I have no choice but to take the risk. And in any case, if Mother Artigas dislikes the idea of the carnival, you can be sure she'll have other reasons."

They finally heard the school bell ring and they parted company, walking toward the study hall building. Merceditas had dropped the mango in her skirt pocket; she could feel it swing there against her leg, and enjoyed its perfume of roses like an anticipated banquet. When she arrived at her seat she took it out surreptitiously and hid it at the bottom of her desk.

Merceditas Cáceres and Carlotta Rodriguez had become good friends in a short time. In truth, one couldn't find two students more unlike each other in the whole school. Merceditas came from a landholding family who owned some of the most fertile sugarcane valleys on the south of the island, as well as the mill after which she had been named. The Las Mercedes Sugar Mill was nearly as large as Snow White Mills, the huge sugar complex of the western town of Guamaní. She had been brought up by English governesses until she entered the Sacred Heart as a boarder; she had few friends and had always led a lonely life, having permission to leave the school only on weekends, when she was driven up the mill's slope in her family's limousine.

She had many cousins and relatives and had hardly had any contact with the people of the town. Inside the mill's compound there were several sundry and utility stores, a drugstore, medical offices, a swimming pool, and tennis courts where her cousins played daily with one another. Merceditas's shyness was in part the result of her not being used to talking to strangers, but it was also the outcome of the Cáceres's unpopular image in Santa Cruz. They had refused to belong to the local casino and *paso fino* club, for example; and their huge fortune had led them to feel a certain mistrust, and in some cases even disdain, of the townspeople. The latter responded in kind, and would never invite the Cáceres to the political and social activities that went on in their homes; an exile that the Cáceres undoubtedly welcomed, since they would seldom bend down to dealing with local authorities at the municipal level for the problems of their sugar empire, resorting always to the central sources of power on the mainland. When they were accused of having no patriotic spirit and of being citizens of nowhere, the Cácereses would laugh wholeheartedly, throwing back their blond heads (of which they were inordinately proud, attributing them to a German ancestor) and claiming that, in fact, the accusation was correct, as they considered themselves to be citizens of the world, and the only good thing about Santa Cruz was the highway that led to the capital.

Because of these reasons every Friday afternoon, when Merceditas left the Sacred Heart, she would lean curiously out the gray velvet-curtained windows of her family's limousine, observing the houses of the town attentively and wondering what life would be like inside. In spite of her great efforts to make friends with the classmates whom she knew lived in these houses, she had had little luck. It had only been on meeting Carlotta that she had for the first time felt appreciated for her own self, without her family name being in the least important. Carlotta's conversation, always peppered with jokes and mischievous innuendos, both cheered and amused her, and she found it especially interesting when she spoke to her of the town.

Carlotta, for her part, had discovered in Merceditas a valuable ally. Her presence in school, unthinkable a few years before, had been the result of the new outlook the nuns had been forced to adopt, when they discovered that the school's enrollment was only half full. It was an expensive academy, and the economic difficulties that even the most respectable families of the town had begun to encounter had forced them to begin to send their daughters to less exclusive establishments. The nuns had then altered their policy of admission, and for the last few years the daughters of the Acuñas, the De la Valles, and the Arzuagas had been obliged to share their top-rank education with the daughters of the Rodriguezes, the Torreses, and the Moraleses.

Among the latter Carlotta had always stood out for her friendliness, although the shade of her skin condemned her, even among the "new" girls, to a relative isolation. She was the first mulatto student to be admitted to the school in its half century of existence, and her recent admission had been talked about as something unheard of and radical even by the families of the "new." The surnames of the recent upcoming elite were still tottering insecurely in the social registers of the town, and this caused them to be undecided as to whether they should assume the canons of purity of blood that their peers, the old aristocratic families of Santa Cruz, had so zealously defended in the past. Thus they chose, in those cases that were unfortunately more obvious, to adopt a benevolent, distant attitude, which would establish the priority of the "mingled but not mixed."

It was true that Don Agapito Rodriguez's considerable assets had contributed greatly to the democratization of the admission requirements of the academy, so that now the venerable Ladies of the Sacred Heart would risk even the admittance of Carlotta Rodriguez to the school. Don Agapito was a small dry goods merchant who had recently struck it rich with a chain of supermarkets that had modernized the shopping habits of the town. In his establishments one could now choose all kinds of fruits and vegetables, as well as dairy and meat products brought from faraway towns or imported from the mainland, so that all the corner vegetable and neighborhood meat stores had been forced to close down. He was a widower, and his daughter was the apple of his eye. All of this added to the nuns' good fortune at having her with them. He had persuaded the owners of the town's food markets to provide the convent's modest daily staples, the dried beef, tripe, and pig's knuckles with chickpeas they so enjoyed, at half price; a visit to the town mayor, his second cousin, produced considerable savings in their electric bill; a call to

Don Tomás Rodriguez, chief fireman and his uncle, yielded
the promise that a modern water heater would soon be in-
stalled at the convent, the cost of which Don Agapito was
willing to foot.

The nuns were congratulating one another for their wise
decision in admitting Carlotta to the academy when they
noticed that an unexpected friendship had begun to bud
between her and Merceditas Cáceres. They always strove to
be together—in the garden at recess; in the classrooms and in
the dining room; and they had had the good luck to have
been assigned neighboring beds in the boarding-student dormitory. At first the nuns were concerned that Merceditas's
family might disapprove of such an intimacy, but they soon
realized their fears were unfounded. The Cácereses spent
their lives commuting from the island to the mainland in
their plancs and yachts, and Merceditas's friends were of little
concern to them. The girls' friendship, on the other hand,
offered the nuns the opportunity to make Carlotta feel accepted and loved at the school, thus partially allaying her
loneliness. For Don Agapito, his daughter's friendship with
no less than Merceditas Cáceres was undoubtedly a blessing
from heaven. The school parents had traditionally attributed
a great deal of importance to the social relations that were
established between the girls at the school, since they often
served as a base for favorable future business transactions,
and in some cases even for unexpected betrothals. (Don Agapito
might perhaps have been thinking of Merceditas's many brothers and cousins, in the case of Carlotta's possible future visits
to the Cáceres home.) The nuns believed, in short, that the
generous Don Agapito very well merited the friendship that
had sprung up between his daughter and Merceditas; as to
the Cácereses, who never cared a fig for the welfare of the
town, and much less for that of the school, they deserved
fully whatever harmful social consequences the girls' rapport
might bring.

Having vanquished the obstacles to their friendship, the
girls spent the year in happy camaraderie, and were waiting
for the day when they would graduate together from the
Sacred Heart. Merceditas had confessed to Carlotta that it

was very important for her to graduate with as many honors as possible, because a high academic index would mean a scholarship, which would permit her to continue her studies at a university on the mainland. Her parents had made it clear that they would pay for her education only as far as high school, since at that time a profession was considered superfluous in a girl of good family.

Merceditas had nightmares every time she considered the possibility of having to stay buried at the mill's compound, married to a second cousin and enslaved to household chores, spending her free time running back and forth after a stupid ball on the family's green clay tennis courts, surrounded by equally green cane fields. She thought of Mother Artigas's offer to help her acquire a grant on the mainland as her only ticket to freedom, and because of it she had put heart and soul into her studies all year.

Carlotta, for her part, had no intellectual ambitions, but she knew that graduating from the Sacred Heart could open many future doors for her in town, and she thus tried to do her best. She knew that knowledge had a practical value, and she hoped, with her newly acquired training in mathematics and science, to help her father in his campaign to modernize the town. She admired Merceditas greatly, her dauntless daring in whatever project she undertook; and she looked to her as her saving Nike. All through the year Merceditas had taken her under her wing, and no one at school had ever dared call her a disparaging name, which might remind her of her humble origins.

Carlotta's good-natured ways, on the other hand, would act on Merceditas like a balm. She amused her endlessly with stories of Santa Cruz. She would describe the sunbaked streets one by one, shaded by groves of honeyberries and centuries-old mahogany trees, although a subtle ironic tinge would always creep into her voice when she talked about the nineteenth-century mansions of the patrician families of the town. She liked to point out that these houses, with white-washed façades heavily gessoed and hung with garlands, amphorae, and plaster cupids, reminded her of a row of wedding cakes just out of the oven and set on the sidewalk to cool. She also talked about the lives that went on behind their walls with a good-natured lilt of reproach, describing, without the merest hint of hate or resentment, how their inhabitants lived eternally in the half-light of respectability, hiding the fact that they were forced to live with much more modest means than those which the opulent walls of their mansions proclaimed to the world.

Thanks to Carlotta's stories Merceditas began to find out about the history of Santa Cruz. The old bourgeois families' proud stance before the economic ruin that the arrival of the troops from the north had provoked at the turn of the century seemed to her quixotic, but worthy of respect. The town's prosperity had hinged on the importance of its port, which had been praised by General Miles after his regiment of volunteers from Illinois had landed. It was blessed by a jetty and a deep bay, which had served as a stimulating rendezvous for commerce all during the nineteenth century, since it offered protection to the many vessels that sailed for Europe and North America, loaded with coffee, sugar, and tobacco.

The mountain range that surrounded the town to the north and to the west had been profusely planted with coffee and tobacco at the time, which the small landowners of the region would transport to the coast in mule trains, to be shipped abroad. Sugarcane, on the other hand, was grown in the lowlands, and it spread over the valley of Santa Cruz like a rippling green mane. Santa Cruzans were at that time a proud people, and they boasted that their coffee, tobacco, and sugar were famous all over the world for their excellent quality. They had, furthermore, made wise use of their bonanza, and with the revenues had built elegant theaters, plazas, loggias, a horse-racing track and a dog-racing track, as well as a splendid cathedral, whose towers could be seen gleaming arrogantly from far out at sea because they had been carved in silver.

All this began to change, and was still changing, with the arrival of the armies from the north. With the ruin of the tobacco and coffee plantations, the farmlands on the mountains were abandoned, and the trading firms that had dealt with them in town were forced to foreclose. Many of the criollo-owned sugar mills had then passed to form a part of the three or four super mills established on the island with the aid of foreign capital, as had been the case with Diamond Dust, the De la Valle family enterprise. Some of them, however, had managed to survive the crises thanks to their ingenuity, and such was the case of Las Mercedes Sugar Mill. More than twenty years before, the Cácereses had decided to build a rum distillery. At first it was no more than a rustic evaporating still, one of the many illegal contraptions that had sprung up by the hundreds in the back patios of the old mills of the valley. The Second World War had begun, and the veterans from Santa Cruz were returning home by the hundreds, armless and lame from its bloody battles, and looking for a magic balm that might make them forget their sorrows. It had been this sorry spectacle that had given the Cácereses the brilliant idea of naming their rum Don Quijote de la Mancha, as the islanders would immediately identify the beaten, half-starved gentleman on the label with the ravaged pride of their own country.

And it wasn't just amid the island's war veterans that Don Quijote's popularity became rampant; it also began to sell surprisingly well on the mainland. The inhabitants of the Metropolis had acquired a taste for the exotic rum produced by their colonies, and they felt inordinately proud of it. Don Quijote became proof that they were becoming internationally sophisticated: from now on, France could well have its Ron Negrita distilled in Martinique, and England its Tio Pepe packed and bottled in Dover, without worrying them in the least. They had their own Don Quijote, who would conquer the world from the lanky heights of his scrawny steed.

With the profits from the fabulous sales of their rum, the Cácereses built their family compound in the vicinity of the mill, turning it into a modern village. The houses all had swimming pools that shone like emeralds under the noonday sun, as well as manicured tennis courts. The atmosphere was refreshingly informal, in contrast to the stuffy customs of the town, where women would never be allowed to go out in pants "tight as sausages," as the Spanish priest used to shriek from the cathedral's pulpit on Sundays. While the women of the town were often overweight and never did any exercise, alternating between the church and the kitchen, where they were the fairy godmothers of their family's pampered appetites, at Las Mercedes women wore white shorts and tennis shoes, played badminton, skeet, and tennis, and would make a daily ritual of tanning themselves half-naked next to their pools.

During this same period Santa Cruz became a skeleton town, and quietly folded upon itself the exuberant flesh it had previously exhibited to the world. The magnificent buildings of yore, the theaters with Greek porticoes and the plazas decorated with fountains, had fallen into disrepair, so that they stuck out in the noon heat like the mysterious bones of a dream, monuments of a past whose practical use could only be guessed at by the townspeople. Sliding like shades at the back of their palatial houses, however, the old aristocratic families still survived, concealing their hurt pride and poverty behind their ornately decorated balconies.

This picture of Santa Cruz that Carlotta painted was a revelation to Merceditas, who had lived until then a sheltered life in the midst of her family's greenbacked cane fields. As she listened to her sitting next to the Grotto of the Virgin of Lourdes, or during their strolls through the school's garden, she was surprised at her love for the town. Carlotta's interest in the old aristocratic families was mainly romantic in character. Like her father, she believed in progress and wanted to participate, once she had graduated from the Sacred Heart, in the town's political and civic development. Don Agapito was an active member of the board of directors of the municipal hospital, as well as of the state penitentiary, and he strove for progressive measures such as importing the latest cancer-treating equipment with federal aid, or adopting a more humane policy toward convicts. He was also manager of the Little League baseball team and an influential member of the Chamber of Commerce and of the Lion's Club, from whose boards he always encouraged the admission of new, energetically active members, very different from those aristocratic gentlemen who had been on the board till then and who lived

as recluses in their own homes, dreaming of the glories of
yore while the town went on dying around them.

Only once a year did Santa Cruz allow itself to return to
the past, and it was at carnival time. As far back as anyone
could remember, Juan Ponce de León's carnival had been the
preeminent social event of the town. King Momo, conga
dancers, demons, and ogres could change costumes but would
always remain the same; to take part in the carnival as one of
these popular figures needed no special voucher, no official
investigation as to family and ancestors. When it came to the
select company of Juan Ponce de León's retinue, however, it
was a different matter. To qualify for the role of gentleman,
with the right to wear a breastplate, plumed casque, and foil,
one had inevitably to be an Acuña, a Portalatini, or an
Arzuaga. In the specific case of the queen, the central figure
of the celebrations, the requisite of social decorum was considered to be almost sacred. For this reason a committee of
worthy citizens was elected every year, who took pride in
selecting an adequate sovereign.

Once the court was assembled, after careful consideration
of all the candidates and a disputed voting campaign, the old
aristocratic families would throw themselves body and soul
into the proceedings, ready to astound once again the inhabitants of the town with the pageantry of their timeworn
riches. Each year they would pick out a theme from colonial
times, as for example the buccaneers of Sir Francis Drake,
who had once boldly roved the island's coasts; or the tragic,
unfortunate visit of Sir George Clifford, Count of Cumber-
land, to the fortress of El Morro, where he had lost seven
hundred men before stealing the organ of the cathedral and
the bells of all the churches of San Juan; or, as in the case of
Carlotta's court, which was to be selected for the feasts of
1955, the heroic exploits of Christopher Columbus.

Perched as a child on her family's modest balustered balcony, Carlotta had been present at many of these carnivals.
From it she had often admired the slow, stately carriages as
they rolled before her house, heaped with calla lilies and
roses and powdered with gold dust, on which rode the members of Juan Ponce de León's court, the children of the

Acuñas, the Arzuagas, and the De la Valles, pitilessly distant
in their disdain for the world and wrapped in their diamond-
studded mantles like immemorial insects that anteceded history and defied the ravages of time.

Mother Artigas was wandering up and down the study hall
aisle at sewing class, keeping watch of the rhythmic rise and
fall of the girls' needles as they flew like tiny silver darts in
their hands, when she suddenly came to a stop. She noticed
an aroma of roses nearby and, joining her hands severely
under her shoulder cape, she carefully scrutinized the faces
around her. She noticed that Merceditas's cheeks had suddenly become flushed, and she walked slowly up to her.
"Would you be so kind as to open your desk top?" she
asked with a smile, leaning attentively toward her, but taking
care that the fringe of her veil wouldn't graze the girl's
shoulder.
Merceditas felt tempted to look at Carlotta, but she controlled herself. She fixed her gaze on the heavy black beads of
the rosary that hung from Mother Artigas's waist. She lifted
the lid slowly, exposing the desk's contents: books, soap dish,
folding glass, sharpened pencils, blue apron, white veil and
black veil, neatly rolled next to each other. Mother Artigas
reached into it with her hand, as though pursuing, with the
sense of smell transferred to the tips of her fingers, the scent
of the Columbus's kidney. Her sense of direction was accu-
rate: she lifted the black veil and there it was, round and
exuberant, giving off its secret perfume in all directions. She
gave her a surprised look, a smile still playing on her lips.
"It was a present from Carlotta, Mother; the committee
offered it to her on a silver platter at the luncheon where she
was elected carnival queen. If you'd like to taste it, I'll slice
you a piece."
She trusted that Mother Artigas would be lenient with her.
She knew there was a law against bringing fruits into study
hall, but it wasn't a serious offense.
"You did wrong to accept such a gift," whispered the nun
haughtily. "Now you'll have to live with it until graduation

day." And, turning her back on Merceditas, she walked rapidly away.

Mother Artigas's beauty had a great deal to do with the authority she wielded at the academy at the time. She had one of those translucent faces in which the lack of cosmetics emphasized the features' perfect harmony, and her exquisite breeding and courteous ways gave proof of her privileged upbringing. Tall and limber, she would appear in hallways and classrooms when it was least expected, and the students would all rise immediately and curtsy before her. Her black canvas half-boots, carefully dusted by the order's sisters at dawn, and her black gauze veil scented daily with lavender, seemed to be everywhere at all times, as her shadow could be seen gliding through the house like a mournful willow's.

In contrast to most of the other nuns, Mother Artigas had been born on the island, and because of her native upbringing it was considered she could deal more effectively than her companions with whatever problems of discipline the students might have, since she could understand them better. The girls were, after all, just ordinary misses from well-to-do families; but once they graduated their social status would become something very different, since as alumnae of the Sacred Heart they had the right to expect the highest respect and esteem of the town.

Most of Mother Artigas's companions had been born in far away foreign cities such as Valparaiso, Cali, and Buenos Aires. Their sad, polite manners, as well as their nervously fluttering eyelids, betrayed the reasons that had brought them to Santa Cruz, where they had taken refuge behind the solid colonial walls of their convent, trying to forget their own worlds in a small, anonymous Caribbean town. Under their tucked wimples they hid endless bitter disillusionments, romantic as well as economic, and their personal dramas were probably a symptomatic sampling of the difficulties Latin American patrician families were going through at the time. The landed aristocracy's tragic fate seemed to be sealed by industrial development, military dictatorships, and the gradual disintegration of a Latin American national consciousness among the new well to do.

Imprisoned in their memories, these nuns shunned an everyday reality that they found increasingly disagreeable, and they did their best to forget, through prayer and meditation, that they were living in a mediocre town inhabited by a people whose customs seemed so difficult to understand. Their entrance to the convent had been a hazardous enough ordeal, having had to raise two thousand dollars, the dowry one was obliged to bring to the altar as a bride of the Sacred Heart at the time, with great personal sacrifices. Once the wedding had taken place, they aspired only to the peace and forgetfulness they felt was their due, submitting without complaint to the strict rules of the convent, which required the virtues of silence, anonymity, and indifference to the world.

In their eyes, the girls that swarmed daily into their classrooms like restless swallows had neither face nor name, but were rather hosts of souls. They knew that, at any minute, they'd be forced to abandon them, since in obedience to the iron regulations of the Mother House in Rome, nuns were not allowed to remain in the same convent for more than three years. For this reason they saw them flock into their classrooms not as girls born in a particular country or educated in a specific cultural tradition, but as the daughters of all and of none; and they willingly surrendered the thorny duties of discipline and ethical instruction to Mother Artigas.

There was an additional circumstance that had conferred on Mother Artigas the mantle of authority in the nuns' eyes. It had been thanks to the generosity of the Artigas family, who thirty years ago had donated their old colonial palace to the Mother House in Rome, that the convent had been founded in Santa Cruz in the first place and that the privileged daughters of the town's bourgeoisie could study today at the Sacred Heart. Mother Artigas had an untiring amount of energy, and under her baton the school hummed like a well-trained orchestra. At dawn she'd already be standing at the kitchen door, ordering the sisters to baste, broil, and roast, with economy and wisdom, the simple fares that would be consumed at the convent during the course of the day. She'd also taken over the complicated duties of laundering

and ironing the sacred altar linens as well as the girls' bed
linen, taking scrupulous care that no fragment of the sacred
host should fall carelessly among them; she personally super-
vised the starching of the nuns' dozens of veils and habits,
ordering them to be dipped in lye once a month to prevent
lice and vermin from multiplying inordinately, and hung out
to dry on the roof under the noonday sun, so that from afar
the convent often resembled Theseus's ship, with black sails
unfurled by Caribbean winds. In short, she took care of
everybody and of everything, and she would claim with
pride that she did it all because the house was so close to her
own heart.

Mother Artigas had had no difficulties in paying the dowry
of two thousand dollars that made it possible to enter the
order. Her family had been, and still was, one of the most
powerful in the country, related to the De la Valles on her
mother's side, and her parents had moved to the capital a
long time ago. She had received an exceptional papal dispen-
sation when she had taken her vows that exempted her from
the cruel law of resettling every three years in a different
country. To compensate she had promised herself, at the
moment of becoming the bride of the Lord, when the priest
was about to crown her head with the resplendent veil of
chastity, to abide unfalteringly by the rest of the convent
rules, casting off all human affection from her soul and
tending only to that future moment of absolute happiness
when she would be admitted into His embrace. She felt so
deeply grateful for the privilege of remaining on the island
that she swore she'd never fall victim to fond attachments,
tendernesses, or endearments toward her fellow human beings,
which became treacherous pitfalls of the will.

For this reason she regarded all display of emotion, all
devoted attachments that might spring up among the girls, or
between the nuns and the girls (the convent's sisters didn't
count because they were of humble origin, and thus even
though they cooked, ironed, and laundered, they were invisi-
ble to Mother Artigas), as a sort of scandal. In her eyes
affection, devotedness, or even friendship were all suspect
emotions that attempted against that sole union, perfect and

irreversible, which would one day take place between the
disciples of the Sacred Heart and their future husband on
earth.

Since Mother Artigas had been named Corrector of Discipline, she had implanted a strict system of vigilance in the
school. In every classroom, in every green-shuttered hallway,
in every dusty path of the school's garden down which the
students ambled at recess, she had posted an eagle-eyed,
vigilant nun, whose black veil clouded all laughter and turned
the girls' amicable conversation into frightened whispers. Her
idea of discipline would change drastically, however, whenever she met Merceditas Cáceres, for whom she felt a special
fondness. Merceditas had been a model student during her
three and a half years at the school, and this made her
inordinately tolerant and understanding toward her. Mother
Artigas held high hopes for her, and she liked to supervise
her studies personally. She had had an extensive education
and had acquired more than one doctoral degree at foreign
universities. She believed that women had an undeniable
right to knowledge, having been unjustly barred from it by
men for centuries, and the only obstacle that for a while had
made her hesitate on her decision to enter the convent had
been the clergy's traditional feminization of ignorance. She
herself had at one time wanted to become a writer and had
played with the idea of challenging the social and literary
conventions of her world that condemned women to silence
or, what was worse, to euphemistic, romantic verses, chock
full of ruby bleeding hearts, cooing love affairs, and lace-
flounced babies, but that hadn't the slightest notion of history, politics, or science. She had by now renounced her
fantasy of a literary life, but had stuck to her guns in certain
aspects of it even after entering the convent. She thus had
always displayed the utmost disdain for the joyless writing of
mystical nuns, whose ultimate role was submission, and she
never encouraged the students to read a sacred book, be it the
Imitation of Christ or *Lives of the Saints*.

Mother Artigas would spend hours with Merceditas poring
over books and explaining to her the most difficult problems

of calculus, philosophy, and linguistics. She always insisted
to her that learning could be a higher goal than bearing
children and that discipline was thus a necessary evil, because it taught people to forgo the comforts of the body and
the pleasures of the senses for the good of the spirit. At these
moments she insisted that the Greeks had only been half
right, and that they would have earned themselves a lot of
sorrow if their approach to life had been to have a Spartan
mind in an Athenian soul. She therefore insisted that, in her
future writing at least (Mother Artigas hoped that one day
Merceditas would become a writer), she never accept the
dictates of male authority and that, be it in politics, science,
or the arts, she always looked to her own heart.

Mother Artigas, in short, believed that the only way women
could dedicate themselves to the pursuit of knowledge was by
forgoing human love and dedicating themselves to the divine
order of things. She was an ardent soul, inspired by the zeal
of her vocation, and she often talked to Merceditas about the
spiritual advantages of deserving a destiny similar to that of
the Princess of Cleves. Her tongue was soft as silk, and her
protégée loved to listen to her when she talked of spiritual
things, feeling from time to time the urge to follow in her
footsteps. Mother Artigas talked to her then of the Sacred
Heart's "burning flame, in which the believer must purify his
soul, before arriving at the divine union with God," and she
encouraged her to alternate her studies with frequent visits to
the school's chapel, where there were always pious ceremonies going on. For Mother Artigas, religious indifference was
the most dangerous sin, because it landed the larger part of
humanity in hell. Merceditas tried to heed her counsel, and
she made a conscious effort to take part in the frequent
novenas, rosaries, and benedictions that went on daily at the
chapel. She even began going to communion at seven o'clock
in the morning every first Friday of the month, because the
nuns had assured her that whoever managed to do so for nine
months in a row was guaranteed salvation, but she found it
more and more difficult to remember, and when she arrived
at the fifth or sixth month she inevitably forgot about it, and

found herself sound asleep in bed. This inexplicable weak-
ness became an obsession with her, and when the situation
had recurred half a dozen times she had to face the possibility
that perhaps she was not meant to be saved. Kneeling next to
the other students at her bench in the chapel, she would then
listen desperately to their whispered prayers and fervid chants,
letting herself become faint under the clouds of incense and
the perfume of the lilies that thronged the altar, only to arrive
at the conclusion, wiping her bloodless brow, that if salvation
couldn't be earned by doing good deeds but only by praying,
she didn't stand a chance. They could torture her knees all
they wanted but not her mind, because she couldn't stand
being bored.

In spite of Merceditas's sincere admiration for Mother
Artigas, something in the nun had always made her keep her
distance. Perhaps it was the perfect beauty of her face or her
exquisite manners at dinnertime, but the nun had always
made her feel a certain apprehension. Since Carlotta's arrival
at the school a year before, moreover, Mother Artigas had
shown herself more reticent in her expressions of affection, as
though she resented the fact that Merceditas now had a close
friend. For all of these reasons, during her three and a half
years at the convent Merceditas had hovered like a moth
around the nun's incandescent allure, feeling at times attracted and at times repelled by her presence.

Thus she wasn't really surprised at Mother Artigas's cold
tone of reproach on the morning she discovered Carlotta's
mango hidden in her desk. She kept quiet, and she did
exactly as she was told. She laid the fruit at an angle at the
end of the writing table, so that the drops of syrup that ran
down its skin wouldn't stain the other objects that were kept
there. At first Merceditas didn't quite understand the extent
of her punishment and she reveled in the fruit's aroma, which
seemed to her an unmerited reward. She would look at it
from the corner of her eye as she wrote her assignments,
read, or sewed, secretly enjoying the fact that the mango
reminded her of her friend, and finding a funny resemblance
between its heart-shaped, golden silhouette and Carlotta's
burnished cheeks.

The fact that Carlotta Rodriguez was elected carnival queen
didn't take anyone in Santa Cruz by surprise that year, with
the exception of the nuns of the Sacred Heart. Don Agapito's
influence had already spread to wider circles, and several of
his friends had been elected committee members of Juan
Ponce de León's feasts. Carlotta, on the other hand, had
always dreamed of being carnival queen, and she jumped at
the chance she was being offered. A few days after her
appointment Don Agapito came to the convent and asked the
nuns to give Carlotta permission to leave the school every
afternoon from three to six, so she could attend to her carnival duties.

Once scepter and orb were held firmly in hand, Carlotta
threw herself into the planning of the feasts. She met daily
with her aides at the casino, from where she announced, as
part of the updating of the celebration, that from then on the
students of all public and private schools, and not only the
children of the bourgeois families of Santa Cruz, could participate in the carnival ceremonies. Everything went well and
a good number of boys and girls, many of them the children
of Don Agapito's friends, had begun to turn up at the casino's door, asking to be admitted to this or that cortege, when
Carlotta's enthusiasm for the celebrations began to make her
feel the arrangements were inadequate, and that enough wasn't
being done.

Set on giving the occasion an even greater luster and a
truly international renown, she decreed that there be not just
one, but three parade floats for her retinue to ride in, which
were to be built according to the exact measurements of
Christopher Columbus's galleons, the *Pinta*, the *Niña* and the
Santa María, and which were to slide over a runner of blue
silk that was to be laid down all along Ponce de León Avenue, bordering the harbors of the capital like a streak of ice
next to a wind-tossed sea. She took it upon herself to supervise the opulent decoration of the costumes to be worn by her
entourage, and she designed her own queenly robes herself,
for which it would be necessary to melt several trunkfuls of
coins worth a pirate's ransom. She ordered, on the other

hand, to give the carnival a more popular appeal, that the
orchestras play only guaracha and mambo, banishing the stiff
cadences of the *danza* and the waltz to the depths of Lethe;
and she commanded that the food that was to be served at the
feasts should all be of Creole confection, perfumed with
thyme, laurel leaf, and coriander, and braised in the ancient
wisdom of kinki fritters gilded in lard. The coronation ceremony, which was to take place after the traditional two-
orchestraed ball, would not be celebrated within the revered
hall of mirrors of the casino but in the middle of the town
plaza, where Carlotta had ordered her throne be set up.

When Carlotta's plans became known, Don Agapito's enemies, the old artistocratic families of the town, began to
complain that the carnival was turning into a grotesque affair
and that it was no longer the elegant social event that it had
been in the past. Their dignity wounded because their children's surnames would not be paged out loud at the casino's
doors at the beginning of the ball, and horrified to think that
they would have to parade down Ponce de León Avenue in
their jeweled attire, easy prey to street hoodlums and an
envious rabble, they began to take them out of the corteges
and forbid them to participate in the celebrations.

When Carlotta realized that her courtiers were abandoning
her and that the carnival would have to be canceled if not
enough young people participated in it, she immediately took
action. She had the walls of the town plastered with edicts
that announced that, from that day on, not just the children
from the Sacred Heart, from Saint Ignatius's, and from the
French Lycée were invited to the carnival, but *all* the young
people of the town, whether they could afford to go to school
or not. The very next day a motley crowd of suspiciously
bedraggled courtiers and duennas began to mob the casino's
doors, gentlemen and ladies decked out in cardboard cuirasses,
tin-foil crowns, and crepe-paper trains who had begun to
pour out of the town's ramshackle slums, as well as from its
impoverished middle-class suburbs, and they were all admitted into Carlotta's court.

At the convent Mother Artigas had finally succeeded in a
campaign to expel Carlotta Rodriguez from the Sacred Heart

as soon as possible. She argued that Carlotta's behavior in the
carnival's planned activities was an insult not only to the
school but to the social class to which she so desperately
wished to belong and for which she was carefully being
groomed. The debate had been a prolonged affair, which had
taken place behind closed doors in the impregnable secrecy of
the cloister. At first the nuns had refused to listen to Mother
Artigas's arguments because they were concerned with the
adverse economic consequences they would have to face if
Don Agapito were to withdraw his generous subsidy to the
school. They reminded Mother Artigas that the world had
changed drastically in the last ten years, and they insisted
that the school's requirements for admission be flexible enough
to accept the fact that Santa Cruz's society was in a state of
flux, so that today's nobodies might be tomorrow's dons.
They mistakenly believed, furthermore, that Mother Artigas's
scruples against Carlotta were based on moral grounds, and
that she had been scandalized by the daring design of her
queenly robes, which had been recently published in the
town newspaper, and thus they had tried to humor her out of
her old-fashioned prudery, pointing out the fact that today
the students of the Sacred Heart all wore plunging necklines
at parties, innocently baring breasts and displaying their legs
under the sweeping, bell-like crinolines of Luisa Alfaro and
Rosenda Matienzo, the town's most fashionable designers.

Mother Artigas's arguments for expelling Carlotta, however, were devastating and final. She pointed out to her
companions that Don Agapito's behavior in the feasts' arrangements had left much to be desired, and that he was
indulging his daughter in an uncalled-for Asiatic splendor,
spending an extravagant amount of money on her wardrobe
and on her orphaned court. As a result of such excesses she
had heard that his business, a chain of local supermarkets
called The Golden Galleon, would soon be declared bank-
rupt. The nuns discussed between themselves, in frightened
whispers, the ominous implications of such a scandal, and
concluded that Don Agapito's economic ruin could bring
about a serious loss of the academy's credibility in banking
circles, as well as its eventual disrepute. Faced with these

possibilities, the nuns voted unanimously to expel Carlotta Rodriguez from school. This was to be done as prudently as possible, as soon as Don Agapito returned from a trip abroad of several weeks. Carlotta would be sent home for a few days, with the excuse that the recent feverish round of activities had made her look peaked, extending her absence until it became final for reasons of health.

It's probable that nothing extraordinary would have happened and that Carlotta's expulsion would have gone practically unnoticed if it hadn't been for the striking metamorphosis she underwent at the time. She had always abided by the convent's rules in dress and appearance, so that when she walked in the study hall with her face smeared with makeup for the first time, the nun who was patrolling the hallways thought it was a joke. She quietly called her aside and asked her if she wasn't rehearsing for her role as carnival queen somewhat prematurely, and ordered her to go to the bathroom to scrub her face.

Carlotta obeyed without complaint and returned to her desk with face sparkling clean. But meekness could become, in her case, a powerful weapon, as is often the case with gentle souls. As soon as she found herself alone the next day at recess, she took out a stick of mascara, a lipstick, and a tube of heavy pancake makeup, and applied them generously to her face. Her features, shaded by the thick layers of paint, acquired a grotesque aspect that, as Carlotta later told Merceditas, laughing, was in character with the savage nature of the mestizo women with whom Juan Ponce de León probably fell in love. It was because she was their direct descendant that she painted her face with burnt coal, corozo nut oil, and the juice of the achiote seed, to test the courage of those not yet respectful of the island's way of life. She had piled her hair on top of her head in a wild cathedral of curls and thus ambled absentmindedly among the students, adorned with bracelets and necklaces that jangled on her white organdy blouse with heretic dismay.

Wherever Carlotta went there was laughter and fingers pointing her way, so that the school was in a constant turmoil. The nuns tried everything in their power to put a stop to this, but to no avail. Carlotta proved equally indifferent to rebuffs and reprimands, and continued smearing her face with paint and adorning herself like a harlot. Since her father was still away, moreover, she couldn't be sent home to stay. It was at this point that Mother Artigas decided to intervene, forbidding everyone in the school from talking to Carlotta, under pain of expulsion.

Final exams were drawing near and Merceditas had begun to prepare herself in earnest. She needed to concentrate more than ever on her daily tasks in order to graduate with honors, but she found it difficult to accomplish. She was always keeping an eye on her friend, who would spend her days silently ambling down the school's corridors, naive and grace-less as ever and with her face now disfigured by layers of horrid makeup, and it seemed to her Carlotta was trying to prove something she couldn't understand.

Although she didn't dare to defy Mother Artigas's prohibi-tion by talking to her in public, Merceditas would always save her a space next to her at the dining room table and the chapel bench, and did her best to prevent the other girls from pushing her out of the school games at recess. Carlotta be-haved as though nothing extraordinary was going on. She kept silent whenever she was ill treated and smiled good-naturedly at everyone, even when she was denied permission to go to the bathroom or to have a drink of water.

"I'd like to know why you're doing this, the point of the harebrained hairdo, of the stuff smeared on your face," Merceditas said to her one day when they were far enough away from the watchnun not to be overheard. "Why the gypsy bangles, the whore's love beads, the floozie rings?" She was angry at her friend, but she didn't dare mention the rumors of expulsion that were flying around the school. She hoped Carlotta hadn't heard them, because she couldn't be-lieve they were true.

Her questions went unanswered, and her friend's silence was magnified by the screams of the girls playing volleyball nearby. A shadow of resentment crossed Carlotta's face, but she soon got over her dispirited mood.

"As soon as Father returns from his trip I'll be going

home," she said gaily. "You have no idea how many things
still have to be done before my coronation! But I promise I'll
come back to see you graduate."

Merceditas pretended she hadn't heard her. She had always thought that if Carlotta was expelled she'd leave school,
but now she knew she didn't have the courage. She just
couldn't leave after so many years of struggle. After all,
Carlotta seemed to be taking everything in stride and not
letting the disgraceful events get her down.

"If you come see me graduate, I'll go see you crowned,"
she said to her gamely, but without looking into her eyes.

Merceditas began to realize the full implications of Mother
Artigas's delayed sentence around that same time, three weeks
after it had been enforced. The fruit, which at first had so
delighted her, had begun to turn color, and had passed from
an appetizing golden brown to a bloody purple. It no longer
made her think of Carlotta's smiling cheeks, but of a painfully battered face. Sitting before it during her long hours of
study, she couldn't help being aware of the slow changes that
came over its skin, which became thick and opaque like a
huge drop of blood. It was as though the whole palette of
colors in the passage from life to death had spilled over the
fruit, staining it with cruel misgivings.

The thought of the fruit began to follow her everywhere,
like the cloud of insects that flew about it at noontime, when
the heat became unbearable. She'd think of it at recess, at
breakfast and dinner, but when she saw it most vividly was
before going to sleep at night, when she lay down on her iron
cot at the dormitory. She'd look then at the ghostly reflec-
tions of the canvas curtains separating her sleeping alcove
from that of Carlotta's, swinging heavily in the moonlit breeze;
she'd look at the white pewter washbowl and at the water jug
standing on the night table; she'd look at the black tips of the
lookout's boots posted behind the breathing curtains, which
reminded her of a snout in ambush, and she could hear, in
the still of the night, the mango's slowly beating heart.

At that time Merceditas also began to notice a strange
odor, whenever she walked into a classroom, or when she
stood in one of the school's winding corridors waiting to be

summoned by the nuns. It surprised her that she was holding her breath at breakfast, before the cup of fragrant hot chocolate the sisters served her every morning; when she knelt on her bench at the back of the chapel; even when she was taking a shower. It was an uneven smell, and it reached her at unexpected moments, when she was least thinking about it. Carlotta had noticed it, too, and had asked Merceditas if she knew where it came from, but she hadn't been able to answer. They had agreed, however, that it seemed to become stronger whenever a nun was nearby, as if the smell had a mysterious association with the morbid exuberance of their veils.

It was Carlotta's cheap perfume that brought Merceditas out of the dangerous melancholic state she was in, on the day Don Agapito was supposed to come to pick her up at the school. She stopped reading and looked at her friend in surprise. It was strictly forbidden to change seats at study hall time, but Carlotta behaved as if rules had ceased to exist. Made up and scented like a street tart, she sat at the desk next to hers and, instead of whispering, began to talk in a normal tone of voice. The lookout's furious glance and the neighboring students' mutterings left her unmoved.

"Are you coming to say good-bye? Father's downstairs waiting in the car, and everything's ready. I just have to go up to my room to get my suitcase. If you like, you can help me bring it down."

Her voice was steady but her cheeks were trembling slightly under the heavy coat of makeup.

"All right; I'll go with you," answered Merceditas, as she put away her book and swiftly lowered the lid of her desk, to prevent her friend from noticing its tomblike aspect. She went out to the corridor and Carlotta stayed behind a few minutes, to say good-bye to several of her classmates. She peered out sadly through the green-louvered windows at the courtyard, and wondered what Carlotta would do now that she wouldn't finish high school. She told herself that perhaps it wouldn't make much difference, and that knowing Carlotta, she'd probably find something in which to make herself useful in no time at all. Her friend lived in a world in which action was what mattered, action that eased other people's sufferings in particular; while she lived in a world of thought. All week she had dreaded the moment of saying good-bye, but now that it had come she felt almost relieved, convinced that her departure was for the better. She felt sad, and she knew she probably wouldn't see Carlotta again for a long time, but she welcomed the thought of having peace reign once more at the school, so she could go back to studying. Above all, she'd be free from the ominous feeling she'd had all week, that something terrible was going to happen to her.

They went up the spiral staircase together and quietly entered the senior dormitory on the third floor. Carlotta took her suitcase out from under the bed and emptied her drawers into it, stuffing in everything as fast as possible. She talked constantly about trivial matters, and her voice had a defiant ring to it, as though willfully breaking the silence that enshrouded the room. Carlotta's voice had a strange effect on Merceditas, who had been used to talking in whispers and walking on the dormitory floorboards always on tiptoe. She looked at what surrounded her as though seeing it for the first time: the heavy canvas curtains, now drawn back toward the walls to ventilate the room, revealed to her how near her own bed had been to her friend's, and hers to those of the other boarders. The night table, the water basin and the jug, the crucifix and the chamber pot, repeated again and again the length of the room as if reflected in a double mirror, made her feel everything was happening in a dream.

Talking and laughing at the same time, they picked up the suitcase between them and began the long trek to the school's main entrance on the first floor. Taking each other by the arm, they flew down the spiral stairs and, a few minutes later, were crossing the green-louvered dormitories of second and third year on the second floor. Once on ground level, they passed the laundry rooms and Merceditas saw the sisters bending over their ironing boards and cement sinks full of suds, pressing and scrubbing altar cloths and bed sheets; they passed the chapel and she saw several of her classmates kneeling in their benches amid clouds of incense, monotonously repeating the same chants and prayers. She saw class-

rooms, corridors, cloisters, classmates all fly by as from a
great distance. Carlotta walked calmly beside her, as though
she had managed to rise above everything. She went on
talking animatedly to Merceditas, and reminded her of the
date when the carnival's feasts would begin. She had never
mentioned the true reason for her departure, and she insisted
she was grateful for the opportunity to devote herself entirely
to her coronation duties.

They were walking now more rapidly, crossing through
the galleries that opened onto the main classrooms, when
Merceditas gave a sigh of relief. She hadn't even considered
how she was going to feel after Carlotta had left and she
would be without a single friend at the school, but she didn't
want to think about that now. Her sole concern was that they
hadn't met anyone hiding behind the classroom doors or
lying in wait behind the corridor's shuttered windows to fling
insults at her as she went by. The girls were all bent over
their books or listening intently to their teachers, and they
didn't even turn around to look at them. She had almost
begun to believe her forebodings were wrong and that Carlotta would finally be permitted to leave in peace, and she
already saw herself saying good-bye to her at the school's
entrance hall, when the smell reached her again. She stopped
in her tracks and put her hand on Carlotta's arm. They saw
them at the same time, standing together in a half circle and
crouching under their somber veils, obstructing the way to
the door.

Mother Artigas stepped forward and disengaged herself
from the other nuns. Her feet slid softly over the slate-tiled
floor, and as she did so her gauze veil billowed around her
like an overcast cloud. Her face, framed by her wimple's
snowy curves, seemed to Merceditas more beautiful than
ever, as though she were looking out at her through a sky-
light. She was smiling, but her smile was an icy wound on
her face.

Merceditas let go of Carlotta's suitcase and warned her to
put it slowly on the ground. It was then that she noticed
Mother Artigas's long Spanish scissors, whose sparkling steel
blades she had confused in the hallway's opaque light with

those of the crucifix she wore on her chest; and that she saw
the second nun, half-hidden behind Mother Artigas's headdress, take a firm step toward Carlotta, holding in her hands
a white porcelain basin. Everything that came later seemed to
Merceditas to happen in a dream.

She saw Carlotta's silky curls begin to fall, still warm and
perfumed, on the floor, and that Carlotta wouldn't budge;
she saw Mother Artigas's alabaster-white hands and arms,
bare up to the elbows for the first time, clipping her friend's
head until she was sheared like a sheep, and still Carlotta
wouldn't budge; she saw her take the sponge the acolyte
handed to her and dip it in the purplish foam of the basin,
which had a pungent smell, and she still wouldn't budge; she
saw her wipe her face with it slowly, almost tenderly, until
the heroic features that Carlotta had drawn over her own
began to fade, erasing her lips and eyebrows, the eyelashes
she had so painfully glued to her lids one by one, her poppy-
red cheeks and her passion-flower eyes, and still she wouldn't
budge.

Struck dumb like a statue, Merceditas listened to what
Mother Artigas was saying; to the stream of curses that flew
out of her mouth in whipping flurries, lashing her friend
with a veritable maelstrom of insults. She was screaming the
dirtiest swear words she had ever heard in her life, such as
"Just who do you think you are, you filthy nigger, you're not
good enough to be one of the convent's cooks and you want
to be carnival queen, stuck up on your throne like a mud-
smeared blackamoor, like the glorified idol of the rabble's
most vulgar dreams! Cursed be the day you first set foot in
our school! Damn the very hour when they brought you here
to be educated, dishonoring as you have done the holy image
of our Sacred Heart!"

As she spoke Mother Artigas tore at Carlotta's uniform,
ripping it apart with her nails while she rained slaps and cuffs
at her bent head. Carlotta, who in her panic had kept the
suitcase clutched in her hand, let go of it at last, and lifted
her arms to protect herself from the shower of blows. The
case fell open, spilling its contents all over the floor. Merceditas
stared at the jumble of clothes, shoes, and books thrown at

her feet and finally understood everything. She approached
Mother Artigas slowly and stopped her next blow in midair.
Mother Artigas turned toward her in surprise, not so much
because she had intervened but because she had dared lay a
hand on her.

"That's enough, Mother," she heard herself say.

Mother Artigas took two steps backward and looked at
Merceditas with all the hate she was capable of. Carlotta
stood between them, her head trounced like a billard ball and
her blouse slashed in such a way that her bruised flesh
showed through everyplace. She was crying silently, like a
huge beaten creature. Merceditas drew near to her and slid
an arm over her shoulders.

"You know what I'm thinking?" she said with a smile. "I
appreciate your good intentions, but it really wasn't necessary. You didn't have to take my punishment home with
you, because now we know for sure where the smell was
coming from." And bending down, she searched in the hud-
dle of clothes on the floor and came up with a stinking,
ulcerated object, which dripped a mournful, tarlike liquid on
all its sides.

"Here it is, Mother," she said, curtsying before Mother
Artigas for the last time. "Here's your Sacred Heart. It's my
gift to you."

III.

ISOLDA'S MIRROR

I.

FROM SANTA CRUZ'S LOOKOUT POINT ONE COULD SEE THE Caribbean shining like a silver knife, where the cane fields died away into the horizon. The air was so transparent that those Santa Cruzans who had taken the afternoon off and driven to the point to enjoy the cool breeze were surprised by the scene before them. They couldn't remember ever having seen something similar: the sky above the industrial complex of the town was absolutely blue, and they said to one another that such a prodigy surely had something to do with Don Augusto Arzuaga's wedding, which was to take place that very night.

For the first time in many years the plant's chimneys had stopped spewing their monstrous plumes of dust into the air, and everyone agreed that Don Augusto had ordered it so, in order for his wedding to take place under a starry sky. Taking advantage of the privilege of their visibility, Santa Cruzans began immediately to spin stories, adding and subtracting details to facts that were already well known to all:

that on that evening of May 1972, for the first time in the
town's memory, the northern bankers and the town's industrialists and businessmen would get together with the old
sugarcane aristocracy of the valley, and they would wine,
dine, and dance under Don Augusto Arzuaga's all-powerful
roof. After a while they stepped out of their cars and sat on
the stony bluffs of the hillock and tried to make themselves
as comfortable as possible under the thin shadows of the
tamarind trees, to enjoy the spectacle going on below.

Above their heads, on the weatherbeaten masts of an old
frigate, swung two bronze lanterns, a red and a white one,
which in bygone eras had served to signal the presence of
pirate ships up the coast. From their vantage point they could
see two very different landscapes. Behind the limestone hill,
in the middle of a spiny tintillo wood, one could see Tabaiba's
rickety huts, painted Mexican pink, canary yellow, and poppy
red by the government as a tourist attraction. The slum had
been there for more than fifty years and had changed very
little, in spite of its recent official beautification: the same
steep, dusty streets that became dangerous mud rivers as
soon as it began to rain, the same noisy pigs, chickens, and
goats scuttling beneath weatherbeaten stilts, the same latrines, built in the past with vats used to store sugarcane
molasses and today with the discarded diesel oil tanks from
the factory; the place had such a picturesque air to it that it
had become a favorite tourist haunt, and many visitors climbed
Lookout Point just to take a photograph of Tabaiba.

From the point one could see people constantly coming
and going down the streets, men and women with bundles of
clothes under their arms, probably the uniforms they would
wear that evening as waiters, cooks, and dishwashers. More
than half the slum would be at Don Augusto's house after
eight o'clock, some having come to serve in the festivities,
some having come to ogle the arriving gentry in front of the
huge iron-lanced gate, some having come to listen, from the
other side of the garden wall covered with purple bougainvillea
vines, to Daniel Santos's immortal songs or to Cesar Concep-
cion's golden trumpet flashing away through the night.

The second landscape unfolded in the opposite direction

from Tabaiba's dizzying cliff. At the foot of Lookout Point, looking toward the sea, lay the town of Santa Cruz, which had changed considerably in the last few years. In spite of the industrial belt that surrounded it, connected to the town by a maze of sunbaked streets, it still offered an impressive sight. In the past the city had been known as the Pearl of the South, and next to the new restaurants, movie theaters, and businesses that had sprung up, its old colonial skeleton stood intact; the old houses of the hacienda owners, with four-foot-thick walls, acanthus-leaf urns on the roofs and putti-holding gessoed garlands over the doors; the red and black stripes of the Fireman's Building, which at dusk resembled a Moorish backdrop for Mozart's *Abduction From the Seraglio*; the monumental pediments of the Atheneum Theater, which was a pompous small-town copy of the Parthenon.

Down these semideserted, semicollapsed streets drove at that very moment an elegant caravan of honking cars, Buicks and Cadillacs of the latest model. In them rode Don Augusto's guests, frantically seeing to the wedding's last details. Driven by uniformed chauffeurs, the cars would stop now before a beauty salon, now before a gift shop or a flower shop, picking up or letting people out, choosing the presents or the orchid corsages that would be worn that evening on kid-gloved wrists and on elborately domed coiffures. The noisy blare of the horns, as well as the mirrorlike gleams of the chromium fenders in the afternoon's blinding sunlight, added to the holiday atmosphere.

From their gray velvet-curtained windows well-to-do Santa Cruzans hailed one another politely, looking around to see who came out of such and such an establishment, which meant he had been invited to the evening's festivities and so would share in the blessings of Don Augusto Arzuaga's generous pocketbook, or who had been cruelly undercut by vipers. It wouldn't be the first time the town had seen such lavishness. Santa Cruz's high society was used to the sugarcane barons' extravagant parties, in which they displayed all the power of their wealth. But times had changed, and with the ruin of the sugarcane industry and the difficult time rum

production was going through their businesses had gone from
bad to worse.

The town's political control at the time was in the hands of
Don Augusto, who could elect whomever he wanted for
mayor or to the town's council. But Don Augusto's industrial
capital had not been solid enough to remain independent, and
he had recently had to borrow a great deal of money from the
County Metropolitan Bank, whose board of directors was
composed of a whole new group of people, energetic merchants, lawyers, and Wall Street investors who had become
partners of the mainland owners of the bank. The sugarcane
barons, on the other hand, had gone from reciting political
speeches with gold pebbles in their mouths from senatorial
benches, dressed in white linen and reveling in Castelar's
oratorial art, to a different kind of prowess. Lighting the
taper on both ends, they had decided to end their lives with a
bang instead of a whimper. They had realized there was no
way out for them and, like the ancient citizens of Rome, had
decided to commit suicide in their own homes, eating and
drinking inordinately what was left of their sugarcane fortunes before their businesses fell into other hands.

The up-and-coming bourgeoisie, the Santa Cruzans who
sat next to the northerners on the board of the County
Metropolitan Bank, on the other hand, forbade their children
to go to those parties, because they were convinced that the
blood spilled by the sugar barons' decision to end it all would
one day fall on the head of whoever dared be present at their
sacrifice. With trembling voices they irately denounced the
communal baptisms in marble bathtubs, into which the sugar
barons would all jump together to revel in the liquid gold of
their rum, with their wives and daughters joining them as
they mimicked the behavior of town prostitutes. White with
rage, they would comment on the sugar barons' indecent
habits, such as the way they had of greeting each other on
the Greek porticoes of their mansions by squeezing each
other's penises under their starched white linen pants, or
their bantering invitations to make love in their snow-cool
sugar depots, sliding down the huge sugar kilns of their warehouses. Or when they drove up drunk through the cathe-

dral's doors, honking the horns of their old, dusty Packards and Hudsons all the way to the altar; or when they swam naked in the multicolored water spouted by yawning lions on the fountains of the town's plaza on moonlit nights. For this reason it had been many years since the children of the new bourgeoisie had visited the houses of the sugar barons, and the same was true of the sugar baron's children, who kept mainly to themselves.

The families of the new bourgeoisie were worried about the disintegrating effect of such behavior on the character of the sugar barons, and they often talked about it in whispers, as if it were a family tragedy. They had arrived at the conclusion that the only way to rid the town of their bad example was to work out a deal with their northern associates at the bank, in which the barons' credit would be strangled slowly but surely. Public opinion was, after all, supremely important to the town's image, and the wives of the bank's executives, as well as of the new young lawyers and merchants, had a great deal of influence in this respect. They had taken it upon themselves to become the arbiters of the town's social decorum, and in their weekly meetings of the Civic Women's Club, as well as in their bridge and sewing parties, they often discussed the need for moral behavior in the bank's clientele. "There have been times," they'd say, "when in the midst of our household chores, perhaps when we were pouring our husband's coffee in the morning or when we sat down in the living room to do the family mending, we had to listen to our husbands tell degrading stories, such as how they had had to deny a loan to such and such, because they had heard he had tried to commit suicide and was now seeing a psychiatrist, or because he had taken his lover to a well-known restaurant, thus defying all the laws of propriety of the town. We're tired of the whole thing, and we think it's time to set a proper standard. The sugar barons may be all the aristocracy you want, but they must be brought to heel." Respectability, integrity, moderation, even the conscientious observance of religious duties thus became the password, the only effective letter of credit for a business venture in Santa Cruz. Divorce, adultery, drunken behavior, and even suicide had become surprisingly less frequent, and the town's churches became unusually well attended on Sundays.

Don Augusto Arzuaga had remained neutral in all this social infighting, perhaps because he considered it undignified to stoop to small-town slander. The bank's local board members and the sugar barons respected him, but he didn't fraternize with any of them because he found it difficult to trust them. The precarious peace that reigned between them, at any rate, had been due to his abilities as referee in the matter, which had kept foreign investors in check until then. In contrast to what had happened at the island's capital, where most of the locally owned industrial complexes had already been absorbed by foreign capital, Santa Cruz's cement factory still belonged to him.

What was most surprising in this whole situation was the fact that Don Augusto and the sugar barons had originally built their empires thanks to those same northerners who now were scrambling to buy everything up on the island. In 1938, exactly thirty-four years ago, Don Augusto had owned a small ironworks, where he had made his living casting the iron horizontal grinders, steel wheels, and winches of the sugarcane haciendas, as well as the steel girders and beams for the arched bridges that began to span the island's river gullies when the northerners began to crisscross it with modern roads. The sugar industry's instability, however, worried him, as the orders he received from the mills weren't always dependable.

One day, in December of that same year, he received a confidential visit from the high command of the northern naval detachment in town. The Caribbean Sea had become infested with German submarines, they said, and they needed to expand their military bases, adding new roads, warehouses, and airports. There was, furthermore, the rumor that Hitler soon planned to invade England, and for this reason it had become mandatory to build on the island a series of huge wharfs, which could at any moment give shelter to the British navy. The naval officers had chosen Roosevelt Roads for this purpose, since the site's coasts could be well protected by the navy from the nearby islands of Vieques and Culebra, thus turning that part of the Caribbean into a small "Mare Nostrum."

"Your island will finally accomplish a heroic role in the war," he was told amicably by the naval officers. "Perhaps because of its strange geological formation, we had never really trusted it before. If you look at it from the west it reminds you of a sheepdog, but from the east it looks like a fish. One could never be sure if it was mammal or amphibian."

The officers had come to Don Augusto with their proposal because his family had been traditionally for statehood. His father, Arnaldo Arzuaga, had emigrated to the island from Cuba fleeing the War of Independence, where most of his family had perished under Spanish guns. Don Arnaldo had hated the Spaniards, and he had had good reasons to do so. He had studied engineering in France, but once he had returned to Cuba, he felt stifled by Spain's backwardness in everything concerning modern building methods and the Spaniard's olympic disdain toward whatever that had to do with technology or science. They were, moreover, a cruel people, and had tortured him on several occasions for being pro-northerner, ripping off his nails with pincers and threatening to drop him in a cauldron of boiling olive oil seasoned with capers.

Ten years after Don Arnaldo had arrived clandestinely on the island, General Miles's fleet loomed on the horizon of Santa Cruz's bay and lined up its guns against the town. An official dispatch to General Macías, captain general of the area, informed him that he had twenty-four hours to surrender before Miles began firing at the town. Macías had initially intended to resist and had gamely deployed his three companies of Hunters of the Motherland on the outskirts, but it had all been in vain. The company was badly outfitted, as the Spaniards had been contemplating leaving the island in the near future, as soon as its recently gained autonomy had become a military reality, and, furthermore, the Santa Cruzans themselves took a decisive hand in the matter. They mobbed the poorly defended Spanish military quarters and threatened to attack en masse if they wouldn't leave town. Don Arnaldo had been at the head of the attack; like most Santa Cruzans, he was convinced that the northerners would bring progress to the island, and he was right. No sooner had the Spaniards left than the northerners began to pour money into it, mapping the virgin forests of the interior, building badly needed roads, aqueducts, post offices, and hospitals, and setting up telegraph lines so that for the first time in history the islanders on the north could talk to those beyond the steep mountains of the south. The Santa Cruzans' enthusiasm at the arrival of the northerners knew no bounds. The bookstores were flooded with orders for English grammars, and they immediately began discussing the possibility of changing the island's name to "Richland," since under the northern flag no one would be allowed to be poor any longer. One of their most radical innovations, greatly celebrated by Don Arnaldo, who had been trained in the Parisian École des Ponts et des Chaussees, had been to put all the towns of the island on the same time schedule. From the day of their arrival, at seven o'clock in the morning, the northern military command began to send telegraphed messages to all the towns telling them to synchronize their pocket watches, so that at noon church bells wouldn't all ring at different times.

Don Arnaldo had profited greatly from all these reforms, and he immediately became a close friend of the army engineers of the sixth regiments of Massachusetts and of Illinois who flocked to Santa Cruz, feeling he was finally in contact with the modern world. His ironworks flourished, he obtained a great deal of business from all the road building and aqueduct planning going on, and he sent his son to study engineering on the mainland. Thus, when the naval officers visited Don Arnaldo and his son Augusto many years later and explained their needs to them, the Arzuagas immediately accepted their offer and agreed to build a cement plant simply for the purpose of furnishing the materials needed for the construction of the docking facilities at Roosevelt Roads. The Arzuagas were the only ones on the island who could help them out, because they had the knowhow to build a cement factory from scratch, without having to depend on machinery that could easily be sunk by German submarines, as it had to be shipped from Europe or the mainland. For this reason, they said, they could have all the credit they needed from northern banks, which would allow them to purchase the site, as well as the equipment and materials needed to set up the cement factory.

When the Second World War drew to a close Don Augusto Arzuaga was already a rich man. He benefited wisely from the building boom that took place on the island in the fifties and sixties, being a peace-loving and civilized man. His dream had always been to build an art gallery for Santa Cruz, so that the inhabitants of the town wouldn't have to travel hundreds of miles to see the marvels of painting and sculpture that had so impressed him when he had first traveled to Europe. He had achieved his dream and his magnificent art gallery was already a reality, its marble pediments rising in the midst of Santa Cruz like a modern Greek temple, undeniable proof that man's spiritual values could be built on science and technology's solid rock, when calamity threatened to strike. The oil market had plunged and the cost of electricity on the island, where everything, even oil, had to be imported, had tripled. There was no way Don Augusto's fortune, no matter how large, could stand the expense of operating his cement factory, as cheap cement imported from other Caribbean islands began to flood the market.

It was because of the above situation that Don Augusto Arzuaga's marriage to Adriana Mercier, a nightclub singer and fledgling classical pianist, was expected to have such awesome consequences. Sitting on the rocky bluffs of Lookout Point or under the cool shade of the rustling tintillo and honeyberry trees, the citizens of Santa Cruz looked at Don Augusto's cement plant under a clear blue sky and commented wonderingly on all these things, asking themselves what would happen at the end of the melodrama.

II.

THE STORY BEGAN THE AFTERNOON ADRIANA WENT TO THE
airport to say good-bye to Gabriel. She was standing at the
gate holding the rose Gabriel had given her in her hand, and
a vague feeling of relief had begun to rise from the soles of
her feet as he walked away, down the narrow corridor lead-
ing to the plane. It was at that moment that Don Augusto
spoke to her for the first time. He had also come to say
good-bye to his son and had been staring at her, with his
gray, languid locks falling over his forehead and his strange
air of a boyish old man. He leaned toward her discreetly as
he put his hat back on.

"I must have seen you before someplace but I don't think
we've ever been introduced," he said with a smile, shrinking
back a bit in his impeccably tailored suit. "My name is Don
Augusto Arzuaga and I'd like to know your name." Adriana
said hello absentmindedly, too pent up in her own self to pay
attention to the old man's greeting.

"Adriana Mercier, nice to meet you."

She was looking again toward the long passageway into
which Gabriel was growing smaller and smaller, his jacket
swung over his shoulder and the wind from the open windows blowing his hair all over the place. She closed her eyes
and tried to smile but felt about to burst out crying. To
conceal it she blinked rapidly, as if something had fallen in
her eye. She could see Gabriel laughing as he stopped and
turned around to wave good-bye one last time before disap-
pearing through the plane's open door. She told herself it was
the smell of gasoline that was making her feel faint and held
on tightly to the package of books that Gabriel had thrust on
her at the last minute because they were too heavy and the
airline official had threatened to charge him overweight when
he had pushed his suitcase on the scales.

It was probably the end. Gabriel wouldn't return to the
island for a long time, and she'd never go to live with him in
Europe as she had promised. She had managed to play her
role to the end and congratulated herself for it; it was better
this way, pretend everything was fine, smile, be affectionate
and avoid the melodrama, the accusations that would later
return to hound you. Let him sail on with his dream, thinking she'd follow him to the end of the earth to marry him,
giving up her career for a family. She wished him good luck
and turned around to walk away when she felt Don Augusto's
hand on her arm.

"You look pale," he said softly, "I think you should sit
down a moment." She let him lead her by the elbow to a
nearby cafeteria where he ordered her a cup of coffee. She sat
before the steaming cup and suddenly felt fragile under the
old man's sympathetic stare, but swore she wouldn't cry. No
sooner had she thought it than two tears began to trickle
slowly down her cheeks. Don Augusto was silent. He took
an enormous linen handkerchief out of his pocket and handed
it to her, spreading its lemony perfume in every direction.

"I thought nobody used handkerchiefs like this any more,"
she said, and tried to laugh as she wiped her tears with it.

The old man smiled without answering. He sat quietly in
front of her, assuming that his presence was more important
than anything he might say at the moment. When she looked

better he said, "You know, you remind me of one of the characters of my paintings. *Isolda's Mirror*. I'd like to show it to you some day."

When she wouldn't look up from the table he added gently, "I don't know what's the matter, but if I were your age, I wouldn't take it so much to heart."

His voice was so sad that suddenly Adriana guessed he had talked to her because of a feeling of solidarity and not, as she had previously thought, for sordid interests. She had noticed him standing apart from Gabriel a few moments before, and they had hardly said a word to each other. It was as though he had come to say good-bye against his son's express wishes. She looked at the age spots on his hands and at the way he sat leaning forward on his chair, as though unsure of his posture, and she thought he must be very old.

"Do you know why Gabriel wanted to leave the island?" she asked point blank, without roundabouts.

"You mean my son? I didn't know you were his friend. He's going to study at the Sorbonne for a few years. Didn't he tell you?" He was silent a minute and then added, "It's truly admirable; the resemblance, I mean. In my painting Isolda is sitting just like you right now, with a cup in her right hand and a rose in her left. My art gallery is in Santa Cruz, you know, where Gabriel was born. It's the most important town on the south of the island."

Adriana got up suddenly from her chair; she didn't want to lose time chattering about an art gallery she had no intention of visiting. She had heard Gabriel speak of the place, which was supposed to be the eighth wonder of the world and his father's obsession in his old age, but she had felt no curiosity about it. She was about to leave when she heard him add, in an almond-oiled voice, "The only difference is that Isolda's cup is poisoned and the rose is a gift of love. She's undecided as to what to do; whether to drink the poison or smell the rose."

She looked at him in surprise. Suddenly she felt aggressive; he probably thought she was a silly girl, heart rent by disillusion; he was probably secretly glad Gabriel had left and everything was over between them. Although she couldn't really be sure he knew they were lovers; Gabriel was very discreet and probably had never mentioned her name to him. He thought they were just friends, which was just as well. She shrugged her shoulders, not wanting to think about it any more.

She picked up the cup from the table to drink the last of the coffee, but Don Augusto stopped her. He took the cup away as though it really did hold poison, and kissed her hand tenderly. "Sometimes it's necessary to believe in love, even if it doesn't exist," he said with a suave smile. Adriana remembered his words for a long time.

III.

SHE DIDN'T THINK OF DON AUGUSTO FOR MANY MONTHS, but one morning she received a bouquet of red roses accompanied by a postcard of a dark-haired woman wearing a choker of coral beads thick as cherries. The woman held a golden cup in her right hand and a red rose in her left, so she immediately guessed who the sender was. On the back was written, in an elegant script. "Will you take a weekend off and come to see my art gallery? I still hope to introduce you to my Isolda some day."

She put the flowers in a vase and stuck the postcard in the frame of her mirror. As she brushed her hair about her head like a black whirpool she looked at her reflection in it and, though she didn't like to admit it, found a resemblance between herself and the woman. The painting bothered her, it was too sweet, almost cloying in its exotic atmosphere. She wondered why Don Augusto insisted on seeing her; maybe he simply wanted to take the place of his son, Oedipus in reverse, to prove his manliness. She didn't really believe it, though. With his millions, he probably had hundreds of women at his feet for whom marrying an old man posed no problems. She turned the postcard around and stuck it back in the mirror, so as not to see it, got up and left the room, slamming the door after her. She went downstairs rapidly to where her car was parked.

She came back at five from the conservatory and met her father coming up the driveway of tree ferns. The ferns he had planted, the driveway he had cleared of vegetation before paving it with asphalt. She opened her purse and took out her keys to open the door, while her father stopped to play with the dogs that had come to greet them.

"I'll help you make dinner if you want me to," he said, kissing her on the cheek. Her father was like that, always helpful, although he'd never let you forget everything they owned, the house, the car, the furniture, was the fruit of military discipline. He got up at five every morning, as he had done ever since he was a sergeant in the army, and at ten o'clock he and her mother were sound asleep, the dogs lying peacefully at the foot of the bed like protective keepers.

Adriana went inside and walked to the kitchen. Before his sickness her father had done many of the household maintenance chores; he had painted the walls, waterproofed the ceiling, varnished the furniture, and weeded the garden and the vegetable patch himself. He had always been feverishly active, as though needing to fight the haunting memory of poverty every minute of the day. Sleeping, taking a noonday siesta, playing the piano for pleasure, were all unforgivable sins to him.

She took down the chopping board from its nail on the wall and heard her father come in behind her. "Sure you don't need any help, darling?" he asked. Adriana felt mortified because he spoke in English. He insisted on doing so once in a while, as though he missed living in the United States. She shook her head and stared out the window at the valley, which had begun to light up as night fell, the glimmer of houses flowing from the dark hills like water. She remembered Gabriel telling her the hills were like her thighs when they were making love, their skin warm and lighted by

golden drops of sweat. She felt a sudden vertigo overcome
her as she thought of him. Her relationship with Gabriel had
always been like that; when she was with him she felt she
loved him, but when he was far away she felt numb, as
though she had never loved him at all. She began to chop the
onion and garlic with a cruel staccato of short stabs, ridding
them of their skins and blinking rapidly to rid her eyes of the
sting that rose suddenly from them.

"We're home now, Dad, you don't have to talk in English," she answered in an irritated tone, which she immediately regretted. Since his heart attack her father was virtually
housebound and could do very little. Her mother went to
work every day as a nurse at the military base nearby, but
her father had had to be commissioned. He did a little
cleaning and picking up around the house, watered the plants,
and waited for the family's return in the afternoon. They had
lived in Europe for many years as a military family, where
her mother had worked as an Officer's Club nurse and her
father had been an attaché to the consular body. They had
visited in Germany, Spain, and Italy, although to Adriana it
had all been more or less the same. The schools she had gone
to in the military bases were all similar to one another, and
English was spoken in all of them.

She began to sing "Noche de Ronda" to herself, opening
her mouth wide whenever she got to the "a" and mimicking
the vulgar, guttural intonation of "The Golden Fat Woman"
in KBM's Tira y Tapate show. Fortunately she didn't have to
spend too much time at home. As soon as she finished
making dinner for her parents she drove out to the city. Then
she began her second life, which she enjoyed much more,
singing at different cafés and bars of the Condado area.
Tonight she'd be working at The Pianola, where her show
would begin around eleven. Tomorrow she'd be at The Grotto,
day after tomorrow at the Easy Chair, and after that at The
Parakeet.

She liked her work, which took her to strange places, to
dilapidated suburbs like the port, always trashridden from
the paper streamers and the confetti that rained down from
the lighted vacation liners docked in its pink wharfs. She had

already received several invitations to sing at important ho-
tels, and she was considering their offers because they paid
well. She knew, ever since she had lived in the United
States, that her physical appearance was attractive to the
northerners because of her smoke-colored skin, her green
eyes, and her fine features, so she knew she could probably
get the jobs. Her favorite hotel, the one she'd really like to
work in, was of course the Condado Vanderbilt, built by the
Vanderbilts many years ago as a French provincial summer
palace. She liked the sight of its blue-tiled ceilings and of its
eaved Parisian garrets rising on the tongue of beach that had
once been sugar-loaf sand and was now a palmed promenade,
which divided the still waters of the Condado lagoon from
the lashing waves of the Atlantic Ocean.

She liked walking down the Condado's sidewalks, full of
honky-tonk shops, electric penises and pink rubber tits, of
hard-core cinemas and gay bars. She had heard that in the
age of the Vanderbilts that part of the city had been known
as The Golden Cup, and that other locally owned elegant
mansions had been built in the vicinity, such as, for example,
the residence of the Brothers Ben, known to citydwellers as
the "Hermanos Brothers," who owned the telephone and the
telegraph companies. At that time the local bourgeoisie had
promenaded themselves elbow to elbow with the Roosevelts
and the Fords down Ashford Avenue, and their children,
dressed in white linen shorts, had played tennis, bridge, and
backgammon in the same courts; they had taken genteel
drives in their Model Ts down the Escambron's boardwalk
and had all dived in the same aquamarine sea before they
realized their expectations were unfounded, and they would
never be invited to their parties. Newport society didn't
simply shun them; it banished them to a leper's fate; it
ostracized them forever from their progressive parties and
their vermouth champagnes. Friendship with the natives could
never be more intimate than a cordial wave of your silk scarf
or of your kid glove from the distant heights of your convertible Bentley or Rolls-Royce. They'd say to each other, laughing, "Just who did those tuxedo-packing monkeys think they
were anyway?" as they called each other up on the telephone,

courtesy of the Brothers Ben. Hurt in their family pride, bruised in the most intricate fiber of their lineage, the local bourgeoise had banged shut the French louvered windows of their mansions and of their clubs and had migrated to the healthier climates of Gardenhills and Gardenville, abandoning the Golden Cup to the northerners.

The area became rapidly dilapidated. Abandoned to the diabolic rust, which rose like a fiery mold from the sea, the houses had begun to burst through the seams of their iron rods so that they looked like overturned umbrellas in the Atlantic wind, their doors banging loose in the night and their windows flapping like drunken gull's wings. Then the carpetbaggers began to arrive, loaded with trunks full of shrill Mexican sarapes and seed necklaces from Nicaragua, to tempt the low-budget tourists who began to travel to the island, the shoe vendors with swollen feet from B. Altman's and Lord & Taylors, the cosmetic peddlers from Woolworth, the Fuller Brush man from Macy's basement shop. These new entrepreneurs began to buy the tottering mansions of the old bourgeoisie, where they set up a string of whorehouses with the teenage girls who were brought clandestinely into the island from Santo Domingo and Haiti. This last innovation was too much for the Vanderbilts, who finally sold their summer palace and left the island. The carpetbaggers turned it immediately into a "ragtime hotel," and it was there that Adriana dreamed of singing some day.

She began to chop the green peppers and went on singing "Noche de Ronda" to herself, now deepening her voice so as to imitate Ruth Fernandez's sexy tone. She closed her eyes and saw herself in a sequined gown going up the stairs of the Condado Vanderbilt's nightclub, El Patio del Fauno, where a fountain spouted pink champagne all night. She walked to the microphone and began to sing *"Luna que se quiebra entre las tinieblas de mi soledad . . ."*

"Please don't sing so loud! I'm watching the last quarter of the Superbowl!" Her father, hurt by her rebuff a minute ago, had taken refuge in the family room and had turned the television on full blast.

"English, English, English! Why must you always speak

English!" she countered, now furiously mincing the sweet chilis, which curled in her hand like tiny bishop's hats. "One must learn to speak English without an accent so as not to be identified, so as not to be singled out!" Her father probably thought she had gone stark raving mad because of her outburst. She wiped off the tears from her cheek and went into the next room, walking up to his chair from behind. She put her arms around him and kissed him on the head.

She had other memories, different from the ones of the military bases in Europe. She could still remember their house in the slum of Bajura Honda, with its slanted zinc roof and its rickety balcony. She had been born in it; and her father had gone there to fetch her and her mother when he had finally returned from Korea, with a steady paycheck to feed them for the first time in their life. On their way to Europe, her father had repeated the same thing again and again, on the airplane, at the airport, once they arrived at the base, where all the houses were the same like in a game of Monopoly: "We must learn to speak English without an accent! We must learn to speak English without an accent!" as though their lives depended on it. He had been surprisingly successful; after a year and a half, no one in Germany or Italy could have guessed English wasn't their native language.

Her father had returned to the kitchen and was sitting next to her on the red wicker chair, reading the *San Juun Star*. Adriana began to fry the onion, and the golden skins of the stove's guardian angel enveloped them in its benevolent cloud of perfume. This time she began to sing a stanza from "La Borinqueña," with an ironic tinge to her voice. "Oh, land of Borinquen, garden where I was born!" Her father smiled covertly, without looking up from his newspaper.

"They say Tavares pilfered the melody from 'The Pretty Peruvian,' " he said craftily, handing her a bunch of coriander so she'd mince it, too. Adriana burst out laughing and gave up.

That night, when she looked at herself in her mirror, she thought her future was anguishingly uncertain. Her father and mother were back on the island to stay, there was no question about it. But it had been a conditional return; they would never belong wholly to the world they had left behind. Because of it they had built their house on a hill, at the end of a winding maze of roads that it took more than an hour to drive through. The house itself was a good representation of their lives. Half rustic chalet, half colonial mansion, it had a Swiss balcony with wooden cutout hearts and a Spanish beamed ceiling, Andalusian glazed tiles in the bathroom, and German iron tiles in the kitchen. Her father never left the house and her mother came down from the hill only to drive to the military base. They lived in an island within an island; they didn't really belong anywhere.

She didn't want her life to be like that. She was terrified by the thought of having to spend her life crossing back and forth over an undefined frontier. When she began her piano studies at the Conservatory of Music she had been advised by her teachers to make her career in Europe; she was a star student, and her talent would be lost on the island. But traveling to Europe was now out of the question, with the family surviving on her father's military retirement. What she made as a cabaret singer was barely pin money. She didn't even know if she'd be able to finish her studies at the conservatory. She desperately needed a grant to pay for her last year there.

She began to brush her hair vigorously, as she did every night before going to bed. When she looked in the mirror she saw there was indeed a resemblance between herself and the woman in Don Augusto's postcard. She took it out of the mirror frame and placed it in front of her. There was something ominous in the way Isolda's hair swirled in a black whirlpool around her face. She left the brush on the table and spread her hair across her own face like a wavering shroud. If she didn't manage to graduate from the conservatory her sacrifice would have been in vain; neither marriage nor career, she'd be sitting on the fence. Staying at home with her parents and helping them entertain their military friends, perhaps finding a husband among them, was not really an option. I could never do it, she told herself, I'd much rather move to a small apartment in town and make my nightclub appearances a career. But she knew that wasn't an option, either; she did it as a temporary pastime, but as a profession it would be suicide.

She was thinking of Gabriel, that she had never heard from him again. She thought of Don Augusto and saw him again as he had been at the airport, standing shyly aside and almost not daring to talk to his son, simply looking at him lovingly and waving good-bye; she saw herself about to faint and Don Augusto making her sit down, trying to make her feel better with his harebrained story about Isolda, the Faerie Queen or the Wicked Witch of the East, about whatever made her think of something else; she saw Gabriel fading away under the dust whipped up by the DC 10's motors; she saw it all in the dark whirlpool of her own hair as she stared in the mirror. The important thing was to be able to make up one's mind, she said to herself; not to hesitate, like Isolda, between the poisoned cup and the rose.

She went to her desk and opened the drawer. She took out pen and paper and began to write slowly, with clear elegant strokes, without stopping to think. Early the next morning she dropped the letter in the mailbox. She had decided to accept Don Augusto's invitation to visit his art gallery the following week.

IV.

SHE ARRIVED EARLY IN SANTA CRUZ. AT THE PLAZA, UN-
der the mahogany trees pruned like gigantic mushroom domes,
she talked to a group of domino players who pointed the way
to the art gallery. It had been a long time since she had last
visited the town; she had been a girl then, and had forgotten
how the heat brought out the profile of things, the brutal
brightness of the sky simmering above like a furnace where
everything, buildings, trees, park benches, people, was slowly
losing its substance, becoming seared into a white-hot out-
line. She missed the cool Atlantic breeze, which at the capital
buffeted the pedestrians' hair and skirts, quickening one's
bloodstream and one's thoughts, and she thought that people
here looked at you with dull, slow-blinking eyes, like lizards
spent by the effort of moving through the dust that rose from
the streets. She accelerated the car and drove toward the
other side of town, where the art gallery was. It was undoubtedly the most imposing building of all, surpassing in
pomp and extravagance all the constructions nearby. It looked

142

like a compromise between a medieval cloister and a Caribbean balcony of monumental proportions.

As soon as she went in the door an air-conditioned gust of air fell on her bare back, and she cursed herself for having worn her low-cut cotton dress of silk-screened red poppies, which was wet with perspiration. She gave her name at the entrance and sat down to wait on a medieval church pew carved with pointed angel's wings. The gallery had a religious air about it; there were red votive candles quavering everywhere and huge flower arrangements on the consoles before the paintings, which made one think of a church. A few minutes later she saw Don Augusto coming toward her down the Gothic arched corridor with a nimble, agile gait that belied his age. He wore an impeccably cut English gabardine suit.

"You can't imagine how I appreciate your having come. Now I'll finally be able to confront my Isolda with her twin, and see which one is more beautiful," he said warmly. "But first I'd like to show you my art gallery."

He took her weekend bag, handed it to one of his bodyguards, and, taking her gently by the elbow, propelled her toward the nearest corridor. They visited several halls, which smelled faintly of incense and in which the old man acted as guide, pointing out the oils, sculptures, and sketches of greater value. Feminine portraits in particular abounded, and there were women of all heights, colors, and ages assembled about, covering the walls from ceiling to floor and looking out from their sumptuous frames.

"Don't you think there are too many of them?" Adriana asked, feeling somewhat dizzy before the wilderness of bodies oscillating before them, nymphs persecuting hunters with baying dogs, princesses taking baths before spying lechers, saints squeezing their hearts out into bloody basins or kneeling in uncomfortable attitudes with a sultan holding a dagger to their throats. The red votive candles, which made the light waver mysteriously around her, added to her malaise. "Maybe you should put some of them away in the basement. It would make the place more peaceful."

"That's impossible, Adriana. Paintings are like people, they need light and air to see and to be seen. Without the light of day a painting dies smothered, and ladies' portraits are the most temperamental of all. They fade, grow scales, shed their varnish like sunburned skin without vitamins. The visitor's eye nourishes their vanity, gives them a reason to go on living. One must be constantly restoring them; cleansing their faces of centuries-old dirt with Castile soap; spreading them on stretchers and tightening their wedges; varnishing and waxing them. My ladies are like divas, they like to be pampered."

Adriana looked at him with curiosity. There was something at the same time jaded and candid about Don Augusto that made him an interesting character. He was probably lonely; she knew he lived alone since Gabriel had left and that he dealt with Santa Cruzan society at arm's length. They went on walking and he began to tell her the story of how he had become an art collector. He had still been married to Margarita De la Valle at the time, who had passed away a few years before. In the beginning she had also been an avid collector, and soon after the war they had traveled together to Europe, where works of art could still be purchased for virtually nothing. They had come back to Santa Cruz loaded with "objets d'art et de vertu" like hunters returning from a successful safari. They had at first decorated their house with them, but with time, as Don Augusto purchased more and more paintings, most of them of nude women (seventeenth-century Spanish, eighteenth-century French, nineteenth-century German, he had no prejudices as to nationality), Margarita began to feel jealous. She got it in her head that Don Augusto cared more about his foreign ladies than about her, and that as her beauty was subject to the ravages of time, she was at a disadvantage. Don Augusto couldn't believe she'd be jealous of the harmless shadows of his portraits, which were several centuries old, or that they could threaten their marriage. In the end, however, he had done as she asked, and the collection was moved to the art gallery. Thus his "harem," as Margarita had called it, was exiled from his official dwelling place. After Margarita's death Don Augusto slept in the house but spent most of his day at the gallery.

Adriana listened quietly to Don Augusto's story. She found his voice soothing and tried not to think about anything. She listened to the gallery's fountains as though in a dream; in every hall there was a marble fountain, brought piece by piece from Europe, and the whole gallery echoed with their cascading waters. Her high heels tapped loudly on the ground when all of a sudden she noticed everybody else was walking on tiptoe. A group of visitors who had come in after them slid by like whispering shades, as though overcome by the spectacle before them.

They finally came to the main hall, where *Isolda's Mirror* was hanging. As elsewhere, the walls were covered by portraits, this time of elegant English ladies by Reynolds and Gainsborough, leaning on ormolu-decorated silk couches and looking very much above all the sufferings of this world. Adriana sat on the side of one of the fountains as Don Augusto walked up to the painting and looked at it reverently. "Here she is. The only woman in the world who makes me absolutely happy," he said with a smile. "I come here every day and look at her; she makes me forget all the family quarrels, all the bad business investments, the aches and pains of my old age. She's perfect; she gives you beauty and asks for nothing in return."

She felt ashamed for having come at all. She'd never have the guts to ask this sentimental old man for the money she needed for her last year at school. She began to play with the white lilies in the water, so she didn't have to look at him. "And she looks just like you, don't you think? The same smoke-tinged skin, the same cameolike profile and rebel locks of hair. Only you should have dressed in hyacinth blue and not in red, because blue is the color of faithfulness." Adriana looked at the painting from up close. Isolda wore an elaborate court dress with a wide, bell-like skirt embroidered with jewels and a plumed headdress. It was in perfect condition; almost as if it had been painted the day before. On Isolda's pink cheek one could see a few faint drops of perspiration. Next to the painting there was a printed explanation of the story: Isolda was King Marco's wife but she had fallen in love

with Tristan, after unwittingly drinking the love potion he
gave her.

"You told me a different story," she said, looking at him
accusingly. "You said the gold cup was poisoned and it
wasn't. Although I suppose it amounts to the same, because
the love potion made her betray Marcos and caused her
death." She was thinking she'd never debase herself, she'd
never ask him for money. "In any case, I don't like her. She's
too stiff, too done up. Her headdress looks like one of your
spouting fountains."

The old man burst out laughing and she saw he had
perfect teeth, pearl white and even. He looked at her admiringly. "You're a real Pandora's box, full of surprises!" he
said, taking her once again by the arm. "A woman with a
mind of her own, ready to stand by your guns. I admit a
checkmate. From now on, I'll never be able to call the Isolda
in my painting the cleverest woman in the world." His eyes
were shining with enthusiasm and, as they walked toward
the door, Isolda couldn't help noticing his pink complexion,
the elegant way he held himself in his fashionably tailored
suit. "Even if the cup holds poison and not a love philter, if
it's solid gold I may drink it after all," she said to herself as
she walked by his side. At the end of the weekend she accepted
his invitation to return to the gallery the following week.

V.

THE FOLLOWING SATURDAY SHE ARRIVED EARLY AND SAT down on the same winged bench. She had dressed very carefully; she wore a wide-brimmed straw hat that became her, and both her skirt and blouse were hyacinth blue. She had even tied her hair back with a ribbon of the same color. She finally saw Don Augusto come down the hall. When he drew near he kissed her hand and murmured with a smile, "And how is Isolda today? Will she be faithful to the end?" Adriana knew he was referring to the color of her dress, but she pretended not to take the hint.

They walked together toward a small door she hadn't noticed the first time, which Don Augusto opened with his key. They entered a beautiful cloister of alabaster columns. A jasmine bush grew against one of the walls, so huge it resembled a green waterfall. In the middle of the garden there was a lily pond, and around it a series of naked statues enjoyed the beauty of their own exposed bodies, either in standing or running poses. A number of gravel paths wound

around the fountain, and Adriana walked down one of them
until she arrived at a small loggia where a lunch table had
been set. Everything had been arranged with impeccable
taste, from the silver-trimmed damask tablecloth to the half-
dozen silver knives, forks, and spoons set on each side of the
plate like a battery of musical instruments. They sat on
golden bamboo cane chairs and drank a toast to their being
there. The glass rang out unmistakably Baccarat. Adriana
couldn't help thinking of the fairy tales she had read as a
child, where tables were served by unseen hands and tablecloths rose into the air by themselves when dinner was over.

"Don Augusto . . ."

"Please don't call me Don; don't remind me of my wrin-
kles, of my gray hair. I'm growing old fast enough as it is."

"Forgive me," she answered in a conciliatory tone. "But
could you talk to me a bit about the reasons you had to build
your art gallery?"

"Man needs more than bread to survive, Adriana. Art, the
same as religion, is a mystery that sometimes had better
remain unexplained, because only as a mystery can it nourish
the soul. Poor Santa Cruzans, the ones who can't afford to
travel and who often go hungry because of our swindling
bourgeoisie, can come here searching for inspiration, to subli-
mate their passions through beauty. I built the gallery for
them, to give them a reason to go on living."

Adriana was silent. She knew Don Augusto was famous
for paying his workers a higher salary than anybody else in
town, and that he had been the only one to fight for the
minimum wage. He had always argued that one day we
would become a state, and that it was better to start getting
used to paying everyone their just desserts, though at present
his decision constituted a bleeding for his enterprise. He had
thought she understood at last the reason for the sinister
votive candles, as well as for the visitors talking in whispers
and walking on tiptoe before the paintings. Don Augusto,
after all, wasn't so different from the men and women who
went to hear her sing at the capital's nightclubs; they needed
drink and music for their romantic dreams; he needed his
paintings for his dreams of human redemption. She took a

long drink from her Baccarat glass and measured her next words carefully.

"It seems difficult to find a reason to go on living simply from looking at a painting, beautiful as it may be. Wouldn't it be better to establish an art academy, where people could learn how to paint, sculpt, even play the piano or the violin? If you did, I'd visit you more often. I only have a year more to go at the Conservatory of Music, but I may have to leave because since my father's sickness we hardly have enough money to get by."

She had finally dropped the bomb. She told herself she didn't care; she'd feel much worse if she hadn't dared say it. She avoided looking into his eyes as she added, "I'm asking the government for financial aid, but you know how it is, they give you so little, it hardly covers one-fifth of the expenses."

Don Augusto looked at her in wonder. "I didn't know you were a student at the conservatory, Adrianita. Now I understand why you have such clear-cut opinions about art. You musn't worry in the least; I'll see to it that the art gallery offers you a loan for as long as you need it."

His use of her name in diminutive touched her. She felt a little spring of happiness begin to flow at her feet, as a cool breeze made her shiver under her hat. She was too proud to be emotional, but she thanked him openly. She had begun to feel at home there, that she belonged. Don Augusto was a generous man, everybody said so. She had heard he had donated thousands of dollars to the university, to the asylum for the blind, to the municipal hospital, to all the charitable institutions in town. And he was an educated man, with very refined tastes. The cloister, the fountains, the flowers that grew everywhere, all breathed forth a cool mist, a delicate perfume designed to preserve the vigor of youth. Before them a broiled lobster surrounded by feathered lettuce leaves curled its pink flesh on a Sevres blue porcelain tray like a clarion of life.

Adriana looked closely as Don Augusto lifted a small, three-pronged fork from the table, and she was about to do the same when a small black velvet case hidden under her napkin fell on her lap. She felt her face redden; it wasn't possible that she should be so naive, so prone to unexpected emotions. "Thank you very much, but whatever it is, I can't accept it," she said in a surprisingly steady voice. Don Augusto lifted his eyes innocently from his plate.

"If it weren't because you look so much like the Isolda in my painting I never would have dared to do it," he said sheepishly, "but I've been carrying it around in my pocket since I first saw you, hoping against all hope that maybe one day I'd see you wearing it. If you don't want it I won't be hurt; it's just a token of friendship."

Adriana took out the ring from its box and held it reverently with the tip of her fingers. "My father couldn't afford even the mounting of this jewel, if he sold everything he had. It must have cost a fortune," she said with an expression of awe on her face. She slipped it on her finger and looked at it more closely. The twenty-carat aquamarine was shaped like a heart, and it sparkled with an icy blue light. "I'd feel like I was carrying an iceberg on my finger, I'd never get used to it." But the stone's soft glow hypnotized her so that she didn't take it off, but went on looking at it from different angles.

"It's like your heart, Adrianita, a drop of clear blue sky. You have no idea how much I admire you for your idealism, for your belief that the world we live in can be a better world."

Adriana began to eat her lobster without taking the ring off, blinking several times to keep away the tears. She didn't know if she was crying because she was happy or because she was angry, but now she'd never go back on herself. She hadn't thought about Gabriel once all week, and that was certainly a change. Don Augusto did her a lot of good; for the first time in a long while she wasn't feeling at all depressed. They ate on in silence without mentioning the ring until dessert came around and another waiter set a pair of tall lemon ice-cloud sherbet before them. It was then Don Augusto broached the question she had been expecting all afternoon.

"Let's get married, Adrianita, let's get married as soon as possible. I promise then you'll be able to study all you want."

VI.

THE WEDDING DATE WAS SET FOR TWO MONTHS LATER, AND Adriana moved to Santa Cruz with her family to get everything ready. Don Augusto's generosity knew no limits; thanks to him her father began to be treated by the best heart specialists on the island and her mother left her job to take care of him. He promised that, once he had seen to some pending business matters in Santa Cruz, they would all move to Europe, where her musical career could finally take off. Don Augusto worshiped her; her merest whim was a matter of dogma to him. If he lived in a world of fantasy in which art had taken the place of religion, that was all right with her. After all, I can help him be happy in life as well as in death, she thought. Our needs cancel each other out, and that's as solid a base for love as any.

Don Augusto had the gardens around his house redone for the wedding. He hired a French architect to build a gazebo, which he called his "Temple of Love," because it housed a marble sculpture of Venus. The sculpture had cold, classical features that could have belonged to any beautiful model, but its body was exactly the same as Adriana's. When she realized this she was surprised but didn't hold it against him. She supposed he had had a photograph of her sent to the sculptor, and had wanted to enjoy the nude statue as a private joke between them. "It's the Venus of Fidelity and I want her to have a place of honor at our wedding," he had said with a twinkle in his eye, ordering the gardener to plant a hedge of blue hyacinths around it. Adriana admired her future husband's daring imagination.

A few weeks after her arrival at Santa Cruz Don Augusto asked her to go with him to his office. They went up the elevator to the twentieth floor and she sat down to wait while he wrote some business letters and called Paris long distance to make an offer on a painting being auctioned. While he was on the telephone Adriana walked to the window and looked out. The view of Santa Cruz spreading before her was depressing. The town's streets looked sad, covered by layers of white dust that swirled in clouds above the trees. She hadn't noticed it before, but now she saw that the dust rained constantly on the town from the chimney chutes nearby.

"It's the dust of progress, Adrianita," she heard him say behind her, as though he had read her thoughts. "It feeds half of Santa Cruz. That dust is worth its weight in gold; thanks to it we live in the modern age."

Don Augusto had taken out a notebook and was slowly going through the guest list for the wedding. "I wanted to speak to you about something," he said. "I know how you feel about it, but it's very important that we should invite the Wall Street partners of the County Metropolitan Bank to our wedding reception." They had discussed the matter of the guests once before and Adriana had said she preferred to have only the family and close friends come to the house after the church ceremony. Above all, she didn't want to have to speak English at her own wedding.

She looked at him in surprise. "I can understand you should insist on inviting the sugar barons, as they are your first wife's kinsmen and Gabriel's aunts and uncles, and perhaps even the businessmen and industrialists from Santa

Cruz, but why must you invite people who don't even live here? I wish you wouldn't do it; I've been a hostess to the northerners all my life at my father's house."

Don Augusto closed his eyes and sighed, leaning his head back on the chair. When he spoke again his voice seemed to Adriana to come from a pit in his chest. He sounded tired and vulnerable; she had never heard him talk like that. "I'm sorry, darling, but it's mandatory that they come. Our marriage has been very controversial in town and I need all the support I can get. The Wall Street bankers have always been my friends, and it's important that they like you. Otherwise, the County Metropolitan Bank may foreclose on our factory's loans.

"It sounds incredible, but I can assure you it's true," he added sadly. "This town's gentry is a nest of vipers, but my northern friends won't let me down."

VII.

ON THE DAY OF THE WEDDING ADRIANA WENT TO THE GAR-
den to make sure everything was the way it should be for the
party. The specially built wooden dance floor was already in
place around the pool, with the orchestra's dais at one end of
it. She sat on a small bench at the edge of the pool and looked
at her reflection in the water. She leaned a bit forward and
remembered the day she had gotten Don Augusto's postcard
in the mail, when her resemblance to the Isolda in the painting had struck her as a quirk of fate. She thought that
everything that was happening to her now had been pre-
dicted by her mirror at the time. Isolda's stunning revelation
today will be very fitting, she thought amusedly to herself.
I'll give Santa Cruzans a surprise they'll remember for the
rest of their lives.

A few weeks before the Wall Street bankers' answer had
come in the mail. They would fly down to the island just for
the wedding; they would be delighted to attend. Don Augusto
had let out a sigh of relief as he handed her the card at

154

breakfast. "As you can see, I can trust my friends. They'll not only come to the reception, but they'll speak up for me at the bank."

The Santa Cruzan bankers had also answered they would come. They had accepted Don Augusto's invitation after a stormy meeting in which their wives had protested loudly, denouncing the marriage as an impudent affair that went against the town's recently revamped standards. The matter was finally voted on, and they had concluded that as Santa Cruz was already painfully rent by the sugar barons' conflicts, the bank would send a delegation of its members to the affair. They were instructed to observe a scrupulously moral attitude at the party, which would put a stop to whatever gossip might arise from their being there as if they approved of the wedding.

Adriana walked away from the pool and began to circulate among the tables and satin-lined chairs to make sure everything was in order. A blue-and-white striped tent had been set up over part of the garden, where the guests would be sitting. She arranged the orchids around the silver candelabra on the main table and she verified that Mr. Harvey, Mr. Wheeler, and Mr. Stanley should sit near the head of the table, near to her and Don Augusto. The sugar barons were all to sit on the left side and the Santa Cruzan bankers on the right. Once she was satisfied with the arrangements, she walked up to the gazebo in the middle of the dance floor, where the Venus of Fidelity stood. A cool breeze began to blow as though it was about to rain, and she went into the house to get dressed.

She opened the door of her room slowly and made sure she was alone before locking it behind her. She sighed with relief; she didn't want anyone to see her wedding attire before the ceremony. She took off her shoes without turning on the lights; she felt so excited she could hardly breathe. She took off her clothes, took a box of heavy powder— "alabaster tone"—from her vanity shelf, and began to powder her body from head to toe. Once she was done, she slipped on the wide set of crinolines she had had secretly made by a seamstress in town and kicked her naked legs a few times under their huge pendulum. She then slipped the hyacinth-blue satin gown over her head, so that it spread over the petticoats like a bell. She next put an elaborate headpiece on her head, a whirling affair of crystal drops and blue sequins, which reproduced masterfully Isolda's medieval headdress. When she had finished dressing she turned on the lights of the room and looked at her reflection in the mirror. She then turned on the tape player to begin rehearsing the waltz. She listened to the music for a few minutes and started to laugh, before she began to dance alone.

VIII.

THE WEDDING TOOK PLACE IN THE MEDIEVAL CHAPEL OF the art gallery. Adriana walked up to the altar to the strains of Monteverdi's "Beata Virgine," played by a monk on the chapel organ. Don Augusto loved her Isolda costume, and made her turn around several times in front of the painting before entering the chapel. "You look magnificent, Adrianita. You make the rest of the ladies, including the original Isolda, look like snuffed-out candles," he said as he kissed her on the cheek before walking with her to the altar.

Once the ceremony was over, newlyweds and guests drove in their limousines to Don Augusto's house. When the receiving line finally broke up Adriana made sure the northerners sat next to Augusto and herself at the table. She guessed they were the only ones who had come to the wedding unarmed. As was the custom in Santa Cruz, the sugar barons as well as the Santa Cruzan bankers had all come secretly equipped with Cobras, Magnums, and .45 caliber handguns, which they wore in armpit holsters or strapped behind their backs, hidden under their impeccably cut tuxedos and dinner jackets.

The Santa Cruzan bankers sat in uncomfortable silence next to their wives who, as they were all dressed in fashionable black, had attracted an annoying cloud of mosquitoes, which whirled above their heads. They refused to drink at all, and kept waving back the waiters with trays of champagne over their shoulders. The sugar barons' wives, on the contrary, done up in faded ostrich feather boas and outdated chiffons, off-the-shoulder silks or plunging tulle gowns, drank and smoked like Cossacks, and chattered constantly among themselves. As the waiters began to serve dinner a minimum of conversation took place between both sides of the table. The discussion, as usual, soon veered toward island politics, and opinions were clearly divided. The sugar barons were mostly for independence, but there was no consensus as to how it should be achieved. Some talked about the "caribbeanization" of the island, by which they meant the Caribbean should really be one country, and the islands should get to know one another better. Some refused to accept this idea, and declared they were the descendants of Spanish hidalgos and had nothing to do with the "niggers" of French- and English-speaking islands who could speak neither French or English correctly. Others, the wildest of them, talked about how Fidel Castro should be approached to help them reach political hegemony. The Santa Cruzan bankers, on the other hand, were mostly autonomists, and heatedly defended the present Free Associated State, as well as its party currently in power. Although no one would have thought of asking them, the waiters, scullions, and maids who served and scurried around them, as well as the pianist, trumpeters, violinists, and even the orchestra conductor standing on the dais would all have been for statehood, so that it could be said that Don Augusto's wedding was a thoroughly democratic representation of the political trends of the island.

Conversation at the table soon became heated, as tension began to mount. Everyone looked askance at Don Augusto, Adriana, and their Wall Street guests, as they talked animatedly among themselves. The rumor had gone about that if the northerners invited Adriana to dance the first waltz, that meant they approved of the marriage, and therefore the bank would have no choice but to condone Don Augusto's new loans. The Santa Cruzan bankers' wives grew angrier by the minute, as it became evident that Adriana and the northerners got along very well together. Sitting tall and straight at the end of the table, with the tails of his tuxedo carefully folded on his lap so they wouldn't wrinkle, Don Augusto enthusiastically toasted his guests. He felt sure that his wife's charm and his northern friends' influence at the bank would solve all his problems that evening.

The orchestra leader announced on the microphone the time had come for the first waltz. The sugar barons and their wives began to walk toward the dance floor, laughing and taking off their ties and sequined evening mantillas because the champagne had made the evening's heat unbearable. Don Augusto was about to take Adriana's hand when Mr. Harvey intervened; he wanted to be the first one to dance with the bride. A surprised murmur arose from the crowd, and the guests all rose to their feet to look at the dancing couple. The musicians wielded their trumpets and trombones on high and Adriana was swept away by the music. It was only after her fifth turn around the dance floor, when the speed of her silk slippers was equal to that of her beating heart, that her jeweled skirt began to rise like a bell, swinging higher and higher up to her knees, to her thighs, to her breasts, held up by her petticoats' hoops. Adriana couldn't stop laughing, and her laughter made the glass beads on her absurd headdress jingle all the more. Suddenly the sugar barons and their wives gave a cry of joy and threw themselves on the dance floor in a pack, by this time taking off their clothes indiscriminately and dousing themselves with champagne, whiskey, and rum from every bottle or syphon available from passing trays. The Santa Cruzan bankers, white with fury, also joined in the fray, so that the elegant audience soon became a mob, a pandemonium of flying fists, handbags, and viciously kicking spiked heels never before seen in Santa Cruz. As bullets began to fly in every direction, Adriana's surprise was finally revealed, that scandalous spectacle which caused not only the bank's ruin, when the northern investors decided to sell their shares and get out of Santa Cruz, but unwittingly that of her husband, as well: the vision of her naked body, an exact copy of the Venus of the Temple of Love, under Isolda's dress. When the waltz was over Adriana realized she was crying, but she couldn't understand why.

IV.
CAPTAIN CANDELARIO'S
HEROIC LAST STAND

THE EVENTS WE ARE ABOUT TO TELL TOOK PLACE WHEN THE Metropolis began to rinse the blood of Saint John the Baptist's lamb off its hands, as it sat gentle and tame on our country's flag. Its senators and representatives were at peace with their consciences and never tried to justify their decision to leave: in recent sessions they had voted unanimously to cede the island its independence. In any case, deep down we had always wanted to be free without daring to be so, and now they were going to help us reach our goal. As the biblical lamb of the Psalms had lain calmly beside the still waters, so had we slept for more than a century under the Metropolis's flag, and it was understandable that now we should be terrified to swim out by ourselves onto the wild, roaring seas.

We would be the first Latin American country to have independence bestowed upon it, and to a great extent against its wishes. In spite of our reluctance, things couldn't go on the way they were, as the Metropolis was tired of being

163

accused of imperialism at the United Nations, where the bloodied carcass of our lamb was frequently thrown at them from the galleries of the Third World. In any case, the senators and representatives said to us, we should be thankful for having enjoyed the privileges of paradise for more than a hundred years, during which we had benefited from the Metropolis's bounties. And it had been all our own fault, they insisted, because during that century we had been the victims of a false national pride, of an insane hubris that now had begun to strangle us like a useless umbilical cord, forcing us to remain forever a stillborn state. How else can one define the Olympic disdain and the boundless greed that had on the one hand led us not to ask for statehood by unanimity when it was still possible, wavering on the perilous swing of to be or not to be before the horrified eyes of the world, while on the other we swaggered and gambled away our souls, persuaded that we were an unseverable part of God's chosen nation on earth, and that we also had an undeniable right to freedom and to the pursuit of happiness?

The sad truth was that for several decades the island of Saint John the Baptist had been costing the Metropolis more than two billion dollars a year in public and welfare funds that would never return to national coffers. In the past the situation had been justified, as the Metropolis's wealth was so great it could afford to turn the island into "the showcase of the Caribbean," a token of their goodwill toward the poor countries of the area. Granted, when it had first taken over the island a hundred years ago in 1898, the Metropolis still wasn't the industrial superpower it was to become during the next century. It had just emerged from the Civil War and was looking for ways to heal the terrible wounds it had inflicted upon itself, and the island's campaign had been a very effective way of doing so. Our islanders had received them with open arms, and the euphoria of seeing our streets lined with people waving the Metropolis's flag and our balconies decorated with flowers in their honor had been a welcome balm for the volunteers from the North and from the South, who felt the sacrifice of war to preserve the union had not been in vain. The newfound pride and confidence in their nation's future had made the soldiers look in horror at the abject poverty of most of our inhabitants, igniting in them a messianic sense of purpose and a generous desire to save as many of them as possible from hunger and disease. Thus, during visits to the island by internationally known figures such as labor leader Vito Marcantonio, and Eleanor Roosevelt a few years later, the world had heard about the distressing state of our people, and their remarks had done a lot to further the cause of our country under the economic provisions of the New Deal. As a result millions of dollars began to pour into the island so that a profound transformation inevitably took place, not only in our outer appearance, but in our soul as well. We no longer knew if we were rich because we had been so poor, or if we were becoming poorer as we became rich, incapable of facing the inevitable fact of our hundred miles by thirty miles of grit that God had seen fit to allot us as our sole heritage upon the face of the earth. Deep down, however, we all knew a day of reckoning would come, and all during that wonderful century Saint John the Baptist's lamb had cowered, terrified albeit well fed, under the terrible shade of the Metropolis's generosity. The year 1998, when Candelario's story took place, saw the realization of that nightmare. At that time the Metropolis's national debt had grown to mammoth proportions, as a result of its unwise involvement in the space armaments race, and it simply couldn't afford to do more charity on the fringes of national boundaries, as charity must perforce begin at home.

Another, less altruistic reason for the drastic paring of the Metropolis's funds that had become mandatory that same year had been the island's strategic geographic location near the Panama Canal. In the past the island had been an invaluable asset for the protection of the Metropolis's merchant ships that traversed the area. For more than a century Saint John the Baptist's lamb, armed to the teeth like Cerberus at the gates of hell, had stood guard in the midst of the belligerent waters of the Caribbean, seeing to it that the oil tankers from Venezuela and Tabasco, the banana sloops from Costa Rica and Yucatan, the coffee freighters from Brazil and Colombia, would all sail peacefully toward the ports of San

Francisco, Baltimore, and New York. But lately the wars in Central America had escalated to such an extent that the protection of the canal zone from land or sea had become a military impossibility. The situation had led the Metropolis to set up a commission to study the matter, and they had come up with the idea of a satellite that could be set in orbit over the area and that would police it with a minimum of expense. The least tactical move against one of the Metropolis's liners would mean instant atomic annihilation for the Caribbean or Central American country that had originated it. Once the problem of patrolling the area had been solved, the Metropolis didn't need the island of Saint John the Baptist any longer, and they had thus decided to abandon us to our long-delayed destiny.

Captain Candelario's story took place a few years before independence became a reality, when our enemies, the party in power at the time, still hadn't been outlawed and we still hadn't won the war. Today we have only one party and, because of the crisis we have been going through, the Constitution has had to be temporarily suspended, but we are finally an independent country. This should be enough to make us happy, but unfortunately it isn't so; there are some of us (those who still haven't been able to adapt) who insist that being independent doesn't necessarily mean being free. This doesn't surprise us; as Plato well knew, the perfect state doesn't exist anywhere in the world, and those who believe it does are usually the poets and dreamers who should be either annihilated or exiled. Captain Candelario De la Valle was one of them. He squandered away his life dreaming of a perfect country where men could both reason and love, not taking into account that reason and love abide in the extreme poles of the soul and can never be reconciled.

The leaders of our party have a clear conscience as to Candelario's death. He died as he would have wanted, and it was thanks to us that he had the brief, gallant end of a hero rather than a long, dishonorable existence. His naked body was found on the sidewalk of Water Bridge the morning after the war between salseros and rockeros finally broke out, when the first official announcement of the island's impending independence had come over the radio. He had been stabbed with an ice pick so many times that his body resembled a field of poppies drying in the sun; and next to him the pavement was strewn with the corpses of dancers, musicians, and Missionary agents lying here and there indiscriminately, with their entrails spilling out like dark bouquets of fading hibiscus blossoms on the ground.

There were rumors that the captain had been betrayed, but they were never confirmed. When violence broke out on the night of the battle, the rockeros didn't strike back but remained paralyzed on the bridge, perhaps hypnotized by the pounding of African war drums and the salseros' monotonous songs, as though they had never heard the captain's order to attack. Thus the rockeros had been caught in a bloody ambuscade and the salsero conspiracy had been surprisingly successful. They had exhibited an unexpected strategic ability and had cornered the rockeros between the condominiums' embankments and the sea, so that the latter had all perished under machine-gun fire. How the salseros had acquired the cunning military knowhow in the maneuvers that led to the onslaught was still a mystery, especially since the captain had remained surrounded by his most trusted agents at all times.

In the court hearings that followed there was one witness who testified as to Captain Candelario's honorable behavior. Lieutenant Pedro Fernández, a Missionary agent and one of the few survivors of the massacre, swore he had heard Captain Candelario give the signal to attack and that he had seen him perish heroically in the midst of a valiant assault of enemy lines. Thanks to his testimony the governor had ordered that Captain Candelario's mortal remains be honored in an official vigil under the Capitol's rotunda, and that he should be buried with all the pomp and circumstance due to a hero of the highest rank, with his medals pinned on his chest like a row of stars. Nonetheless, rumors persisted in the capital that Captain Candelario's magnificent funeral had all been a government hoax.

Candelario De la Valle had been recruited into the party

only six months earlier as commander in chief of a special brigade called the Missionaries, which was to patrol the streets of the city in times of serious trouble. He had graduated a year before from North Point Military Academy as the honor cadet of his class, the only one to receive the rank of captain upon graduation. Dressed and gloved in his gala uniform, with shimmering saber at the waist, blue silk sash across his chest, and the plume of his patent-leather cap blowing whitecaps over his forehead, what he had loved most about the academy had been the courses of military strategy and history, the fencing tournaments and the parades across the emerald green Field of Mars, where he had marched proudly to the rhythm of drums, tubas, and horns. He had just turned twenty-two and martial stalwartness was in his blood; both his great-grandfathers had been men of arms, on his mother's side an English colonel and on his father's a Spanish brigadier. Captain Candelario wasn't at all interested in money, but lived only for honor, dignity, and arduously won glory. With his delicate frame, his plumed cap fluttering in the wind, and the inside of his saber engraved with the motto "*Ad Astra Per Aspera,*" he resembled more a character from one of Jose Campeche's oil-painted miniatures than a military man trained for bloody continental campaigns.

Candelario was a cultured, widely read man of refined aesthetic tastes. He had a very precise idea of the importance of love and war in life; he saw the second as man's most heroic calling and the first as his most sublime, but love and war could be waged only on behalf of a perfect woman and of a perfect country. He still had hopes of finding the former some day, but believed destiny had cruelly swindled him of the latter. On entering North Point Candelario's most revered hero had been Simón Bolívar, but a gnawing conviction of his country's timidity had dissuaded him from following in his footsteps. Bolívar had been born in Venezuela, a rich, powerful land of endless plains and pampas, and he could thus count on its telluric force to ultimately free her of Spanish rule. The island allotted him by destiny, on the contrary, was small and poor, and there was no way Candelario could think of it as great, no matter how much he loved it.

For this reason he had a special place in his heart for the memory of his great-grandmother, Doña Elvira De la Valle, who had also been an incurable romantic in love with her island, and he felt near to such writers like José Gautier Benítez and Pachín Marín. In England his favorite writer was Lord Byron, who had died 174 years before, struggling to free immortal Greece from the Turk's infidel embrace.

Captain Candelario's anguished conviction as to his country's mincing spirit was not only the result of his daily observations, but had also been impressed on him since childhood by parents, friends, and teachers. They repeated day in, day out the same arguments so he should never forget that his minute, delicate island could never become independent. Their Antille, the smallest of the greater and the largest of the lesser, was nothing more than a picturesque goat's dropping, a pigeon's moss-mottled egg, a Hesperides's mythical nose drivel which had magically remained afloat for centuries amid the snow-white breakers of the coral reefs. Their island was a doll's paradise: it had handkerchief valleys, rivulet paint rivers, papier-mâché mountains, brown paper-bag mines, and, as if all that were not enough, it was poised on the verge of one of the deepest underwater chasms of the earth, the Milwaukee trench, and the least tremor of rebellion would plunge it into a twenty thousand mile abyss.

Candelario had, after much soul searching, finally accepted the sensible advice of his peers. From then on he read Gautier Benítez's poems to himself with an even greater passion but with a more doleful accent. Like his grandmother Doña Laura, he loved above all others the verse by Gautier that went: "Everything about you is light and voluptuous,/ Sweet, peaceful, promising and tender,/ And your inner world owes its charm/ To the sweet affection of your outer world." Candelario was convinced that this was the most prophetic verse ever written about his country. It was because of their delicate nature, he told himself, that his countrymen had remained innocent of exhilaratingly brave deeds, ignorant of the elation that gunpowder could produce when bullets grazed one's forehead, or of the joyful trembling of war banners in the wind as one marched bravely behind them. It was for this reason that they had been prophetically awarded the lamb of Saint John the Baptist by Isabella the First, Catholic Queen of Spain, so that they might emblazon their national shield with it, and that the motto *"Semper fides Agnus Dei,"* engraved in a blue silk ribbon, had coiled peacefully around its delicate hoofs for centuries. It was because of this, Candelario told himself sadly, that the party in power, wisely estimating the islander's peaceful nature, had ordered that the lamb of Saint John, which until then had only appeared on the country's official shield, should thereupon become the symbol of its flag.

The party's officials had been right after all. How could a country that was always bleating *"¡Ay bendito!"* at every problem ever become a responsible, self-sufficient nation? The thought used to torture the captain in his sleepless nights, and he never found an answer to the question. Candelario was, in short, full of dreams and noble ideals, but he was a sad young man, and even the heavens above him seemed stifling, less blue and less transparent than those above other countries.

The party had recruited Candelario thinking that the modern war techniques he had learned at the academy would provide the Missionaries with badly needed training, but they made the mistake of not specifying clearly what his duties would eventually be. They took for granted that Candelario would tacitly understand the philosophy behind the new strategy to be adopted by the state, and which *"A Dios rezando y con el mazo dando"* expressed so adequately. Thus he had mistakenly understood that the duties of his Missionaries' brigade would simply consist of patrolling the avenues and streets of the capital, so that order and peace might be restored to them.

Violence and confusion grow rife in uncertain political times, and the island had been no exception. The resolution taken by Congress still awaited the president's seal of approval, so that independence wasn't yet a *fait accompli* and it could take months until the matter was ultimately decided. In the meantime the country had become prey to an unnamed terror, which had begun to strangle it like a noose. For more than a year no properties were bought or sold, the shares of local businesses had taken a plunge, no dividends were declared, and all salaries had been frozen. In his nightly patrol rounds of the capital, Candelario was a constant witness to the chaos: it was at night, when everybody was supposedly sleeping, that the local businessmen and bankers, merchants and professionals, visited their bank vaults to take out their certificates of deposit and their jewelry, which they then secretly transferred to yachts and private airplanes ready to depart immediately for more secure ports. It was at night that the dismantling of the huge tuna canning factory was taking place, as well as of many of the chemical factories and those that built electronic equipment for the defense industry of the Metropolis. Everything that was transportable was being taken apart and hoisted onto the huge cargo ships moored on the ports, so that as he crossed the nearly empty industrial lots in his Missionaries' Jeep Candelario could hear the abandoned chimney chutes and the loose derricks and cranes moaning like phantom organs in the evening wind.

The senators and representatives of the party in power had taken radical measures to end the flight of capital from the island, but to no avail. They didn't have the power, which our party was to acquire later on, to nationalize the banks and prevent anyone from traveling to another country, and so they sat powerless in their capitol seats, under the rotunda that was an exact copy of Monticello's, and watched the country bleed at their feet. The fear that all economic aid from the Metropolis would eventually stop was an even heavier sword hanging over their cowed heads. Even in our midst the pride we felt on first hearing that we would become an independent country had suddenly seemed almost banal, a vain strutting before the thought of possible economic ruin, and if it hadn't been because as party officials independence would also mean absolute power, we would perhaps have wavered in our patriotic resolve. Welfare funds, veterans' pay, highway and home building funds, as well as medical and public school subsidies would all evaporate into thin air. In their official radio announcements, constantly transmitted through Radio Rock and Radio Reloj, the party in power had uselessly tried to address this problem, struggling to allay the panic it was creating among the people by asserting that these Spartan measures would never be wholly acted upon, because they were going to do everything in their power to prevent the Metropolis from giving us our independence. "We must keep our wits and be sensible about this," they told their terrified listeners again and again. "Remember that in the past our country has managed to weather even worse catastrophes, as for example the hurricane of San Ciriaco and of San Felipe, and we have always come out of them with head held high." But the party in power knew their bell was tolling and that independence would mean their political demise.

The party needed someone like Candelario desperately, to put into action the strategy they had finally devised to meet the crisis. They believed the way to prevent the Metropolis from abandoning us was to convince them that we could tighten our belts and do without the economic privileges we had enjoyed until then, as long as our Metropolitan citizenship, and such basic advantages as social security, national defense, and postal services would remain intact. Funds would be eliminated right and left, so that the Metropolis's expenses would be cut by half, and campaigns for island statehood would be banned forever. In a situation like this, it was imperative that law and order be enforced in the capital because this would prove to Metropolitan senators and congressmen that we were willing to meet the challenge, that we were mature enough to accept being poor and live according to our means. Candelario's role would be to see to it that the party's new code of iron discipline was respected by all citizens, in the hope that, impressed by our good behavior, the Metropolis would relent in its terrifying resolution.

Candelario had heard rumors that strife was renting the government apart and that because of it soon there would be a lot of bloodshed, but he didn't believe what he heard. He had accepted his commission on the island gladly, after a painful absence of almost ten years, during which he had studied at several private Metropolitan schools. Now he could prove to himself how much he loved his country, and threw himself heart and soul into his job as commander in chief of the Missionary Corps. On the first day of his commission he noticed a heaviness of mind and body in his underlings that worried him: they all had beady eyes and slaughterhouse arms and shoulders; and he determined they needed to brush up their sense of the heroic, so they would approach war as a sublime vocation and not as a butcher's trade. Almost all the agents under his command were of humble origin, and they had been able to escape the slums' stinking sewers only thanks to their privileged physical constitution, which made them excel in those military activities in which only brute force was needed. For this reason their peers had never bothered to teach them anything else, and they had remained deprived of the more intellectual aspects of the art of war. Candelario was horrified at the inadequacy of his men's spiritual education, for which they weren't at all responsible, and he immediately determined to remedy the situation. He believed a truly great warrior must be a Renaissance man, whose mind had been just as carefully trained as his body, and thus he ordered a whole shipment of books on philosophy, sociology, and the ethics of martial art, which he paid for out of his own pocket. He distributed the books among his subordinates and forced them to soak themselves in Plato, Aristotle, Holderin, and Clausewitz, and to learn by heart the military campaigns of Leonidas, Julius Caesar, and Alexander the Great. As to the physical aspect of their education, Candelario forbade henceforth the use of iron knuckles, razor blades, bludgeons, and machine guns, which he believed only atrophied man's natural defense reflexes. Setting the example of Pericles before them, he reminded them of the effectiveness of Athenian persuasion in the Peloponnesian Wars, and advised them to strive to achieve the enemy's defeat first through intelligent discourse, resorting to a measured violence only in extreme cases, since skillful strategy would always be the more rewarding. He had a gymnasium built for them in the ancient Spanish fort of San Cristobal, and there he urged them to learn the arts of boxing and wrestling, as well as of discus hurling and lightning-javelin throwing, because sports always encouraged a healthy competitive spirit, as well as stimulating conversation on tournament courts.

Candelario considered himself fortunate because, on the first week of his new commission, he had become good friends with Lieutenant Pedro Fernández, the Missionaries' most highly respected man-at-arms. "Let's shake hands, comrade," Candelario said to him when they met, pushing military protocol aside. "I feel certain that working together, we'll be able to train a first-rate military corps." Lieutenant Fernández was a tall, wide-shouldered dark man whose family came from the western town of Guamaní, the same place Captain Candelario's family was originally from.

They both felt a boundless respect for history, as well as for personal courage and honor, which they considered man's supreme virtues. Candelario was a history fan and he could recite the names of the island's three hundred and ninety-five Spanish governors by heart, describing them, undoubtedly with too much idealism, as magnanimous sword-and-cape knights, whose main occupation had been to educate and civilize. Pedro, who didn't share Candelario's pedagogic view of history, for his part felt a greater admiration for the island's Caribe Indians, who had fought the Spaniards tooth and nail and who had been all but exterminated by them. "They were true warriors, masters of the art of war, as well as of the art of sculpture," he would tell Candelario, laughing. "When the *guasábara* broke out, they tied their Spanish prisoners to a log and poured melted gold into their mouths with a funnel, so as to turn them into gold statues."

The fact that Candelario's ancestors had all been people of means and high social standing, while Pedro's had been slaves just a hundred years earlier, didn't in the least affect their newfound friendship. Candelario was Don Ubaldino De la Valle's grandson, the same one whose house had mysteriously gone up in flames on the night his grandmother, Doña Laura, had died. His father, Arístides De la Valle, had sold his share of Diamond Dust Sugar Mills to Snow White Mills, and with the money had moved to the old colonial quarters of the capital, where he had bought and restored an elegant eighteenth-century mansion, with ten balconies of carved wooden balusters and a carriage house. Candelario had been born in that house and, as he was an only child, had been pampered and raised like a prince. In spite of the fact that they had lived in town for almost twenty years, however, the family always considered itself Guamañenan, and Candelario was no exception. Whenever he visited Guamaní he felt as if he had been born again, so happy was he to stroll down its elegant, oak-lined streets.

Pedro, on the other hand, had been born in Finibusterre, Guamaní's most terrifying slum, where the streetwise arts of judo and of gouging your assailant's eyes out at the right moment were as essential as eating or breathing. The slum had once been, under Spanish rule, the hideout of a veritable nest of pickpockets, shoplifters, and miscreants worthy of a Monipodio's court, and had been the nightmare of the Spanish Guardia Civil. In more recent times, however, it had become the favorite settling ground of those war veterans who came back armless and legless from the Metropolis's Asiatic and Central American wars, and who wished to conceal the sad spectacle of their maimed bodies from the prying eyes of the world.

As soon the war veterans began to establish themselves in the area, they renamed the slum Villa Cañona, in honor of those soldiers who had fallen at the front like butchered ewes. The original settlers of the slum, the gay reapers of careless pocketbooks and the entrepreneurs of lucrative whore-mongering, resented the renaming, as well as the ever-increasing presence of battered heroes among them, who sat sunning themselves on their doorsteps with bent heads, sad-dening their once-animated streets with warrior songs. Be-cause of the growing animosity between delinquents and veterans, at least half a dozen shootouts a day took place in Villa Cañona, during which the combatants entrenched their machine guns and automatic rifles behind the thick cement balconies of their houses.

Pedro Fernández had been born in one of those houses that were typical of the slum, built with cardboard boxes, Coca-Cola crates, rusted zinc sheets, and palm tree trunks, but surrounded by a three-foot-deep embattled balcony that turned it into a virtually impregnable fort. Like Candelario, he came from a family of long military tradition, but which had been involved in military action more recently. His uncle, Monchín Fernández, had lost his right eye on Pork Chop Hill, after having downed half a dozen Koreans from a palm tree with his automatic rifle; and his two older brothers had been killed in Vietnam. His father, Juan Fernández, was alive only by chance. He was a twice-decorated Vietnam veteran, a proud recipient of the Order of Merit; during the Tet offensive he had thrown himself into a trench with a live grenade in his hand, after being sent on a special mission behind enemy lines. The government had declared him a hero, and every month he got the highest veteran's paycheck in the whole ghetto, but his wife, Marcelina Fernández, thought nothing of this, and would gladly have done without the money if it had meant having her husband back. Juan, a witty, good-natured man before the war, was now a mound of formless, silent flesh, which had to be wheeled in an invalid's chair around the house.

Ever since he was a child, Pedro had wanted to get away from his family's ill-fated military tradition, and thus had decided very early on to become an athlete. He dreamed of becoming Villa Cañona's star basketball player, as this would permit him to leave the slum, putting the nightmare of the daily shootouts between the gangsters and members of his family behind him. He was undoubtedly well qualified for it: he was taller than all his friends, and his embankment-wide shoulders had won him several nicknames when he had played at the capital, as for example The Watusi and also The Wall. Because of the miraculous speed of his feet, however, which seemed to grow wings as soon as he entered the court, in Villa Cañona he was affectionately known as The Thunderbolt.

Pedro came very near to making his dream a reality. He was a first-rate student and soon won his teachers' confidence at school. When he turned eighteen he won the Roberto Clemente Baseball Grant, for which more than ten thousand public school students on the island also contended. When he was finally chosen, among all the promising athletes who were his same age, to join the island's Olympic basketball team, he became Villa Cañona's undisputed hero, and that night they celebrated by lighting a candle on every zinc roof of the slum. His father, his uncle Monchín, and his many cousins all felt enormously proud of him.

The island's increasingly difficult political situation, however, had thrown the Olympic team onto hard times. Since talks of possible independence had begun almost a year before, the party in power had begun to look on the Olympic team with disapproving eyes. The Olympic team permitted the island to compete as an independent country in the Caribbean and Central American games, side by side with Santo Domingo, Haiti, Cuba, Costa Rica, Honduras, and Mexico, and the party in power feared that this participation might be considered unpatriotic by the Metropolis's congressmen. This wasn't at all the case, and the congressmen were delighted to participate in the games indirectly thanks to their island's "associated state," but as was customary the party in power was more papist than the pope. Its officials began to argue publicly that the island's Olympic team should be abolished, and that if Roberto Clemente had been able to play with the Pittsburgh Pirates for so many years, hitting more than two thousand hits over Pittsburgh's steel-etched skyline, it was inconceivable that younger island athletes shouldn't try to play in Metropolitan teams. For this reason, a few days after he had been nominated to the team, Pedro received an official communication from the party, congratulating him for the honor received but suggesting that such distinctions be sacrificed to the country's well-being. He should therefore renounce his nomination as soon as possible and inquire into joining a Metropolitan team, for which they were willing to offer the highest recommendation. Pedro, however, rejected their offer, claiming he disliked traveling up north where it was always too cold, and that rather than achieving international fame as a Metropolitan big leaguer, he preferred only to be known locally, as Villa Cañona's Thunderbolt.

When they heard of his denial, the party decided to take action. One day, as Pedro left home for the Olympic gym, he was assaulted by a Missionary brigade. They hit him so many times with their bludgeons that they broke both his legs, as well as several ribs and his collarbone. Before they left they looked him over as he lay motionless on the ground. "They won't call you Thunderbolt in Villa Cañona any longer," they laughed, "but perhaps they'll want to call you Thunderstruck." Pedro was wearing the sky-blue rayon gym suit and Star Trek tennis shoes he had always been so proud of, and as he lay there paralyzed he looked at the Missionaries with all the hate he was capable of. He didn't even try to dodge the last of their kicks as he memorized the features of every one of them.

His relatives found him several hours later, lying unconscious on the pavement, and carried him home, but Pedro refused to tell anyone what had happened. He never admitted who had beaten him up, and he became taciturn and silent, hardly talking to his parents. As he lay convalescing in bed he refused to see any of his old friends, and he had his now-useless tennis shoes, which he had strung proudly from one of the bedposts, thrown away. All he did was read the newspapers all day, learning about the party in power's frantic campaign to reverse the catastrophic process of independence. "The party is right," he told his mother while she patiently changed his bandages or helped him move his legs about, encased in their thick plaster columns. "We must do everything in our power to keep the Metropolis from leaving the island. Violence is like fire; it can only be stopped by a greater fire. From now on, if the party decides to eliminate the members of the Olympic team one by one, I'll offer myself to help them do it."

It took Pedro several months to get out of bed, and when he did so he never played basketball again, neither on the Olympic team nor on any of the Metropolitan teams. Although he managed to walk with a limp, dragging his right leg only slightly, running was now out of the question. When he became convinced of his fate, he decided to join the Missionaries' brigade, trying to alleviate somewhat his family's economic plight. It was for this reason that Pedro could not agree with Candelario as to the effectiveness of a more humane military training that gave emphasis to such activities as reading and practicing gymnasium sports, as he had himself lived by the law of the land since his accident and was convinced that "he who strikes first strikes thrice."

Candelario and Pedro had remained very fond of each other, in spite of their differences of opinion. The captain had absolute trust in Pedro and would always ask his advice before making any important decision. Pedro, on the other hand, was a loyal friend, dependable and resourceful, and he helped Candelario out with all sorts of practical problems. He acted as his personal chauffeur, took care that his food should be cooked the right way, had his clothes and shoes cleaned and polished regularly, and even carried his briefcase for him, as he followed him everywhere like a devoted shadow.

Candelario patrolled daily the streets of the capital in his convertible Jeep driven by Pedro. Sitting tall and debonair on the backseat, proud to be wearing the insignia of the golden lamb on his gold-braided navy-blue uniform, Candelario reviewed the panorama of the city with an increasingly heavy heart. The streets echoed with the cries and lamentations of those who were held up at every corner, beaten, stripped of their belongings, and then left on the pavement for dead. Since the crisis had begun, even the most elemental laws were constantly broken; people had ceased to pay taxes, house-to-house postal service had been suspended, and one had to walk to government offices to pay telephone, water, and light bills personally. In addition to these ills, the city had been invaded by a veritable horde of pickpockets, pimps, and drug traffickers, who behaved as though they were its true owners. Candelario had set himself the task of ridding the city of them, but had forbidden his Missionaries to beat up the prisoners whenever their raids were successful, as it had been customary to do in the past. He insisted in personally supervising the operations, to ensure that the prisoners would be treated in a civilized manner. Every time there was a detention he would step down from his Jeep under a boiling hot sun, the insignias on his uniform's lapels about to melt on his chest, and would talk softly for several minutes with the unhappy miscreant. Turning away his eyes sadly under the patent-leather visor of his cap, he would reproach them sternly but cordially for their action, telling them to save their resourcefulness and daring for more dignified occasions, and pointing out to them that by ripping chains, stealing pocketbooks, or holding up drugstores they'd never be able to allay their fear of independence, but were only contributing to the country's chaos and debasing their own souls. In these episodes, however, the miscreant always suffered the same fate. No sooner had Candelario and Pedro left the scene in their convertible Jeep than the Missionaries would let a storm of blows, slaps, and punches loose on their victims, until they collapsed unconscious on the pavement. Railing against the unhappy destiny that had placed them under the authority of a dandified prima donna who forbade the use of iron knuckles, lead pipes, and bludgeons, so that they now had to skin their fists in teaching their countrymen the proverb "the law is best obeyed when written in blood," they would lift up their victim by feet and shoulders and throw him unceremoniously at the bottom of their police vans.

At other times Candelario and Pedro would drive their Jeep through the capital's elegant suburbs, such as Gardenville, La Rambla, and El Alcázar. The spectacle before their eyes was equally chaotic: FOR SALE signs had gone up everywhere, and mansions with swimming pools, tennis and squash courts could be had for a pittance. People could be seen moving out everywhere, transporting their oil paintings, antique furniture, and Oriental rugs into vans, and half the houses had already been abandoned. Leaning toward the front seat of his Jeep, his face pale with badly controlled anger, Candelario then whispered to Pedro that sometimes he felt ashamed of his own kind; whether rumors of impending independence were true or not, running away from one's homeland at the moment of truth was equivalent to treason. It was because of this that he often felt more comfortable with people of humble origin like Pedro than with those of his own social class, since Jefferson's most valid truism had been "merchants have no country." As Pedro didn't answer but kept on driving as he looked sternly ahead, Candelario believed he agreed with him.

The Missionaries were considered a military elite that risked its life daily for its country, and for this reason they would be invited to all the important social functions of the party in power. Candelario and Pedro used to attend these parties together, where many attractive girls would also be present, and where they were flattered and treated like heroes. Both young men stood out at the many gala functions celebrated at the time at La Fortaleza, Casa Blanca, and the Arsenal; Candelario tall and lean, with an unruly lock of blond hair falling over his forehead, and Pedro equally tall although more solidly built, always leaning his mahogany-thick shoulders a bit forward to hide the unevenness of his stride, but keeping himself proudly erect, as though wrapped in the flame-colored war mantle of his Watusi ancestors. Together they offered a striking spectacle that contrasted greatly with the rest of the Missionaries, all brawny men with meatball biceps and pachyderm calves, who circulated among the elegant furniture of the party officials' mansions like bulls in a china shop, and they became immensely popular among the female set.

Instead of feeling satisfied with his romantic conquests at these parties, however, Candelario found them depressing. He was very different from Pedro, for whom love was nothing more than a pleasant diversion, a transient game he had the right to enjoy, after risking his life for his country. Candelario took love seriously, and he just couldn't make advances to this or that society girl without thinking of the consequences. His military training had been so thorough, he had been taught to discipline his mind to such an extent, that he had somehow lost contact with the primeval roots of his body, with that ancient drive which makes it possible for the flesh to keep in contact with nature. He had dreamed so often of the perfect woman, he had drawn her face so many times in his imagination as he lay sleepless on his iron cot, that he felt as if her features had worn away under the darkness of his eyelids. The paradigm of his beloved was so exacting, and on the other hand he was so painfully shy, that his romantic adventures usually ended up in disaster. Every morning, when he performed the ablutions of his gentleman's toilette, he'd look at himself in his small campaign mirror and admire his clean-cut profile, the classical turn of his head, and his delicately drawn mustache, and he'd feel sure that that very same evening he'd find the perfect girl and make her fall in love with him, but when opportunity presented itself, he'd feel dull-witted and bashful. When at the end of a party he'd finally make up his mind to invite a girl up to his apartment, she was the one who had to kiss and embrace him, while he lay dejectedly in her arms feeling like an empty bronze statue. Once the platonic episode had come to an end, the girl would rise from his bed, get dressed, comb her hair, and leave without saying good-bye, as someone who had been invited to dinner and had been forced to fast. For this reason, the girls Candelario invited never wanted to go out with him a second time, and he began to be less popular at government parties. Pedro's case was totally different, and he always had dozens of girls to choose from, as his deformity was considered by them to be an exotic trait.

An event that took place at the time temporarily took the friends away from their romantic preoccupations. Salsa music had lately become increasingly popular in the capital, and its adepts could be counted in the hundreds of thousands. They had become so numerous it was rumored they had lately organized themselves into a party or, as others described it, into a sect, which celebrated its ceremonies and congresses nightly at different meeting places of the city. There was really no basis to believe these rumors were true, but the salseros' popularity was undeniable. It was as if the people, indifferent to the economic chaos that threatened the country, had thrown themselves into a feverish festival of tribal music, so that at night the city's streets resounded with the beating of African drums. The salseros lived in the slums and were mainly a migratory population. They had originally settled in Barrio Obrero, La Cantera, and Los Bravos de Boston when they had arrived from the countryside, fleeing the ruin of the sugarcane, tobacco, and coffee industries at the end of the thirties and forties. By 1950, however, they had realized a second migration was imperative for survival, and thus they had flocked to the mainland by the thousands.

The island had always remained their paradise, and they returned to it periodically, an Afro pick stuck in their red-tinted hair, and wearing the flame-colored T-shirts, polyester pants, and Champion tennis shoes they had bought in the Bronx. They walked into the capital's elegant suburbs carrying their monstrous radios or cassette players blaring full force, and tuned in to all-salsa stations like Zeta 93. Now, at the threat of losing the possibility of traveling to and from the mainland, which permitted them to make a living without losing their homeland, they had become more vocal, and their music voiced their discontent in increasingly radical political terms. The interesting part of this phenomenon was that even though the salsa was identified with slum dwellers and was considered the music of the rabble, it had lately also become increasingly popular in the elegant bars and discos of the city, and was also played in the homes of the upper-middle class, where rock had reigned supreme until then. The rockeros, on the other hand, had their own musical groups, but they had remained apolitical in their songs. They were mainly teenagers dressed in jeans, Playero T-shirts, and designer sandals, wore their hair long and tousled, and in the daytime could be seen windsurfing on Isla Verde beach or listening to stations like Alpha Rock 105 in their sports cars. In spite of its popularity, however, rock had lately begun to lose ground to salsa, and this situation had begun to worry the leaders of the party in power, who disapproved of songs with a political meaning.

In their daily rounds from Polvorin to Fondoelsaco, from Altoelcabro to Altoelcerdo, Pedro and Candelario were witnesses to how the mob kept pouring out of the slums and into the well-to-do quarters of the city, with radios going full blast and singing Ruben Blades's songs. "Life is full of surprises," sang Ray Barreto, as he beat on the congas all the way from Tanca to Tetuan. "The nightingales are singing, a new day is about to dawn," chanted Ismael Rivera's warrior-minstrels, as they played their kettle drums with all their might all the way up Ponce de León Avenue. "You make me feel sorry for you, you really do," sang the band of Celia Cruz, whose grandparents were originally from Mozambique, as they shook their flame-red Afros all the way up Cruz Street.

Candelario found salsa atrocious, but he admired the salseros' courage, their defiance of the party's clearly expressed orders that popular music remain apolitical. And since there was nothing he and Pedro could do to stop the avalanche of singing mobs that walked past them, in his heart he felt secretly happy that, even though his countrymen didn't have the courage to fight for their independence, at least they could sing about it. Pedro, on the contrary, had no aesthetic prejudices against salsa and enjoyed listening to it. He believed that playing popular music was as honorable a way of earning one's living as any other, and in fact, salsa had lately become a very productive occupation, as the concerts brought in considerable sums of money. The salseros, furthermore, sold an enormous amount of records, tapes, and videos, and were looked upon as heroes all over the island.

One day Candelario received a confidential telephone call that had to do with salsa concerts. Several high party officials had become even more seriously worried about them, as they feared they might get out of hand. "We've heard several political terrorists have infiltrated the salsa bands," a cold, impersonal voice said over the telephone. "Can you hear me, Candelario? Do you understand what I'm saying? And as it's impossible to determine which bands are infiltrated and which aren't, from now on it will be your duty, as commander in chief of the Missionaries' brigade, to prevent all salsa concerts from taking place." And as Candelario had remained silent over the telephone, the voice added, "You'd better get the salseros back in hand, Candelario, if you want to keep your job."

Candelario hung up feeling angry. Granted, salsa was vulgar and could hardly be considered music, but many people made a living by it, and to stop the concerts, apart from being an injustice, would be practically impossible. His feelings of pity, however, were soon pushed to the back of his mind when he thought about the consequences of disobeying the orders he had received. He was, after all, a De la Valle, and his family, as well as the circle of his well-to-do friends, would consider it a scandal to be dishonorably discharged from the Missionaries' brigade. On the other hand, he couldn't see himself in any other career but the military. Just the thought of being cooped up in a glass-and-steel cage on the twentieth floor of one of the bank buildings of Hato Rey where most of his friends worked terrified him. He refused to become another small-time business executive, with no other aim in life but to make money buying and selling stocks and bonds on Wall Street, since he had no business of his own. The offices of the bank buildings of Hato Rey were full of the children of rich islanders who, like Candelario's grandfather, had sold their sugar haciendas, tobacco or liquor factories, marketing or construction firms, as well as other types of family-owned businesses to foreign investors, so that now they could really contribute very little to their country's private sector. In any case, the harm to the island had been done a long time ago, when the funds that had poured into it from the Metropolis had made people used to a standard of living they really couldn't afford. Granted, it was a cruel situation to have to take away what one had become used to expecting, and this was what the present curtailing of federal funds boiled down to, but in a potentially explosive situation social order had to be maintained, and perhaps things could be worked out later on, when waters had returned to their normal level. This anguishing situation was what the salseros' songs expressed with unexpected poignancy.

Having reasoned thus, Candelario took it upon himself to put into effect the disagreeable order he had received, and the next day he arranged several punitive expeditions into La Perla, a slum perched beneath the ancient Spanish battlements that surrounded the old quarters of the capital. A number of salseros were taken prisoners and brought to the Missionaries' barracks at San Cristobal's fort. There, in its badly lit medieval dungeons, they were subjected to barbarous corrective measures, of the same sort Candelario had forbidden when he had first taken over the brigade. The expedition was supposed to serve as an object lesson for the salsero community all over the island, and once the miscreants were returned home with bleeding heads and broken ribs, no salsa concerts were given for several weeks, and silence reigned supreme in the shantytown of La Perla, as it clung to the sea-battered cliffs of the ancient city. Perhaps it was this silence, which made Candelario feel increasingly like an executioner, that made him embark on an even more dangerous adventure, though of a different sort.

Every Saturday night Candelario and his brigade would make a tour of the capital's most elegant nightclubs, to insure that salsa wouldn't be played in them again. That night Candelario had walked into Susana's, an exotic disco with glass stalactites hanging from the ceiling and water tanks full of languid fish lining the walls. He looked for a while at the couples writhing on the dance floor to the rhythms of Mick Jagger and the Stones, and sat down by himself at the back of the room. As had been his habit recently, Pedro preferred to sit at the Missionaries' table rather than at his table. A serious argument had broken out between them the week before: during a recent punitive excursion to Guamaní, the Missionaries had gotten a kick out of chasing the salseros all over the zinc roofs of Villa Cañona's huts, and when they had brought them back as prisoners to the capital, Pedro had asked him to set them free. He had several relatives among the detainees: his uncle Monchín and three cousins, who had recently joined the slum's salsa band as horn player, conga player, and percussionist. "They're from our hometown, Captain," he said, feeling confident he would be lenient with them. "I assure you that if they've decided to join the band, it's not because they're terrorists, but because jobs today are hard to get, and they have to make a living."

Candelario, however, refused to listen. It had been a difficult decision to teach the salseros a lesson, and he had been sleeping badly because of it. But making an exception with Pedro's relatives would only make him feel worse. "I'm sorry, comrade," he told him as he gave him a sympathetic handshake. "But at North Point I was taught that the law allows no exceptions." And he begged him not to worry, because once the men had taken their punishment he would take care of them: they would be permitted to join the Missionaries' military band, where they could exchange the common salsa horn for an aristocratic tuba and the barbarous conga skins for a military drum. Furious at his friend, Pedro had reminded him that only a few weeks before he had been making speeches about the humanitarian virtues of dialogue and respect for the opinions of fellow human beings, and he accused him of being a hypocrite, since "it had been necessary to rub his civilized varnish only slightly the wrong way in order for the savage in him to show its head." After this incident Candelario had tried to make up for the beating by personally visiting Pedro's relatives in the hospital and paying for all their medical expenses, but the relationship between the two men had inevitably taken a turn for the worse.

Candelario ordered a whiskey on the rocks from one of the waiters in dragonfly costume who flitted past him. A mob of punk teenagers, wearing Anne Klein jeans and Paco Rabanne shirts, twisted and whirled on the dance floor to the beat of Elvis Presley's rhythms. A group of rock musicians, bending over their electric guitars as if they were machine guns, shouted out their lyrics at the dancers and stamped the floor with their cowboy boots. Suddenly he heard someone speaking behind him.

"What's your favorite music? Is it salsa or rock?"

He turned around toward the darkness behind him and looked curiously at the girl. Even though half buried in shadows, he could tell she was a beauty. "Excuse me, but I didn't hear what you said," he lied.

"Of course you did. You just don't want to admit you heard it. Anyway, you probably enjoy rock. I know you certainly don't like salsa."

"I think you'd better change the subject," Candelario answered sternly, lighting a cigarette and blowing a screen of smoke before his face.

The girl laughed a short, mischievous laugh and slipped next to his seat at the table. Candelario couldn't help admiring her. She had curly red hair held tightly back from her face by an Afro pick, and her breasts were loose under her flowered T-shirt. Because of her appearance, he thought at first she might belong to one of the salsa bands, but he soon changed his mind. She was too white and her diction was too polished to have been born in the slums; she was probably just another rich little girl breaking away from home, posing as a salsera to infuriate her parents.

"I'm a salsa fan. It makes you feel alive, in contact with your cultural roots."

Candelario shook his head and smiled at her sadly. "That doesn't surprise me. Today even the most educated of us have become contaminated by barbaric behavior. Our political independence is threatening us with a second invasion of the Huns and, like the Rome of ancient times, we may soon succumb under their scourge."

"Well, since Barbara is my name, that wouldn't seem so bad after all. Saint Barbara, as you may well remember, is the Missionaries' patron, and her statue stands guard before their powder magazine in San Cristobal's fort. She was the one who turned away Sir Francis Drake's and Sir John Hawkins's twenty-four frigates from the city's port in 1595. The officers had sat down to dinner in the captain's ship, and were about to drink from their beer mugs, when one of Saint Barbara's cannonballs ripped into the room and blew them all to pieces; all excepting Sir Francis Drake, whose high-backed red velvet chair miraculously saved him."

Candelario looked at her admiringly. He could feel only respect for people who knew the history of the island as well as that, since today people seemed to have lost all memory of the past. "Everything you say in your story is true; but is your name really Barbara?" he asked, as he offered her a cigarette.

"No thanks," she said, as she took out a marijuana cigarette from her handbag. "I prefer my own grass, like the lamb on our flag. It may not be my real name, but at least my hair isn't tinted; it's naturally red, like the saint's."

Barbara took a sip from his drink and looked at him curiously and with head askance, sliding her finger lightly over the small gold insignia that Candelario wore on the lapel of his jacket. "Don't you think it's a shame to have a lamb as our country's national symbol? I would prefer a lion." Candelario's face grew red and he took the drink away from her. He finished it at a swallow.

"The lamb is a symbol of peace. Our country has always been a peace-loving nation; that's why we've never needed an army, that's why we've never waged a single war. We've always solved our problems through constitutional dialogue and thanks to our respect for the law. In 1898 we achieved our autonomy from Spain through dialogue, and we'll manage to weather our present difficulties the same way. Violence never solves anything, Barbara, and until the present moment our poverty and our helplessness have been our best allies. No one, not even the Metropolis, would dare wage war against us, because international opinion would rush to our aid. The only way we can perish is if violence comes from within."

He wondered at himself for talking at such lengths with a total stranger, and about things he rarely admitted, even to his own conscience. But all of a sudden he felt better; he had learned something new about himself: that peace was very important to him. He also realized he had been alone for too long and that he needed to talk to someone. He felt the girl's warm knee rub fleetingly against his own and he took out his wallet to pay the bill. He left a twenty next to his empty glass and got up from the table. "Let's take a walk," he said. "We can talk better outside."

Candelario slipped by the Missionaries' table without looking at them, and the girl followed him obediently out of the disco. Once on the street, he took her by the arm and gave a deep sigh. The fresh sea air blowing from behind the old colonial battlements nearby made him feel better; lately he had had to put up with so much: his superiors' brutal orders to crack down on the salseros, Pedro's angry recriminations for having betrayed him and the new humanitarian code he had tried to establish, the Missionaries' sly remarks as to the inconsistency of his methods all put him in a vile mood. He felt violence seething all around him, and all of a sudden he wished he had someone to take it out on, someone he could push around, too, as he was being pushed. As he crossed the street he suddenly realized he was gripping the girl's arm too tightly and that she was squirming away from him. "I didn't want to talk about it in there for fear we might be overheard," he said to her in a conciliatory tone, "but you shouldn't be going on about how much you like salsa. The government has forbidden it, and just mentioning it could land you in jail."

The girl looked at him with fear in her eyes, as she slowly rubbed her arm. Candelario pushed her aside and walked rapidly past her. He had thought of inviting her up to his apartment for a drink, but he felt miserable; he decided to go home alone. It had begun to rain and his building was still several streets away, so he walked rapidly and with bent head under the fluorescent street lights. On each side of the street the sidewalks were lined with huge piles of garbage packed in black plastic bags, ripped open by street dogs so that the cobblestones were strewn with pieces of chicken, rice, bread, empty soup cans. Rats scuttled away on hearing his steps ring out in the dark, and Candelario thought that if things went on the way they were and the crisis continued to paralyze the city's garbage collection, the bubonic plague could well break out once again in the old, embattled city, as it had in the sixteenth and seventeenth centuries, and then the party in power would really have a problem on its hands. He would have given anything to turn back the clock and find himself marching once again at the head of his military cadre, on his academy's emerald green Field of Mars. If anyone had asked him what the purpose of his career was at that very moment, he wouldn't have known what to answer. He felt his return to the island had been a mistake, since it had only awakened a brutal violence in him, and he had never believed in violence for violence's sake.

He turned up the collar of his uniform before bending the corner of his own street, and as he did so he saw the girl was twenty paces behind him. She had wrapped herself in a brightly flowered shawl and walked half-bent under the now-pouring rain, which lashed against the wooden balconies of the nearby houses. When he saw that she was soaked from head to foot he waited for her to catch up. He felt the rain had somehow brought them together, since she probably felt just as miserable as he did. "Would you like to come up a minute to dry yourself?" he asked her politely. "I promise you'll have nothing to fear."

The girl smiled under her rain-tangled hair. "It's not really necessary," she answered. "You looked so sad back there, that's why I followed you." But he insisted and she finally walked up the narrow three flights of stairs to his apartment. The room was large, but Spartan in its simplicity; under the high beamed ceiling there was hardly any furniture and nothing on the walls except for a large poster of Johann Sebastian Bach and another one of Ludwig Van Beethoven hanging on either side of the narrow top-floor windows. Candelario's diploma, framed in gold, hung at the head of the bed.

"You have good taste," said Barbara as she looked approvingly around her. "On your right music's greatest Neoclassic and on your left its most passionate Romantic. You seem to be divided between order and passion."

Candelario laughed and gave her a towel to dry herself as he did the same, stepping behind a makeshift screen to change his shirt for a dry one. He then walked over to a tape player and began to play Haydn's Creation, before serving brandy in two small glasses and putting them on a tray. He felt no romantic inclinations at the moment and simply wanted to sit and talk to her for a while. Because he guessed she didn't agree with his opinions he wanted to explain everything as clearly as possible, and maybe in doing so he could understand himself better. But when he turned around with the glasses he was surprised to see that she had begun to take her clothes off and was walking toward his bed. He had half guessed at her body in the disco's booth, but he was totally unprepared for what he saw; for the two enormous moons that dawned on the pale dunes of her flesh, for the dark triangle of desire that riveted her perfectly rounded torso like a severed star. It had been such a long time since he had made love that he became hypnotized by her beauty, and he began to take off his clothes almost without thinking, as if in a trance. As he lay down next to her he began to feel shy and inadequate once more, and was afraid destiny might deny him once again the elemental pleasures of the body simply because he hadn't found the woman of his dreams, but he soon discovered he was wrong. Barbara's wise caresses soon made him forget military discipline, and he felt as though an ice armor had begun to melt inside him. After a while he saw his penis rise in front of him like the mainstay of a mysterious sailing ship, and for the first time in his life he felt absolutely sure as to who was at the helm. After they had finished making love he fell back exhausted on the bed and sighed. His body felt as if it had floated up from a bottomless pit.

Candelario met with the girl he called Barbara (since she had refused to tell him her real name) almost every night during the following week. She would arrive wrapped in her flowered shawl, smoke a marijuana cigarette in bed, and then proceed to make him absolutely happy for almost two hours. After making love she would get up as if nothing had happened, start to laugh as she began to put on her clothes, and go on laughing as she went out the door. "Dust to dust and diamonds to diamonds," she would say to him teasingly as she said good-bye, meaning that, as Candelario belonged to the De la Valle family, old owners of Diamond Dust Sugar (Candelario had told her about it), he had to think of his reputation above all and probably would never marry her, but simply want her as his friend. She, for her part, had told him about her own middle-class family, and about the way her father, a salesman at a shoe store on Fortaleza Street, had had to struggle all his life to make ends meet.

As soon as Barbara left, Candelario began to feel dejected. He saw himself as a traitor to his heroic ideals, precisely because he was being loyal to his military duties. He still made the Missionaries follow the courses he had organized at San Cristobal's barracks, making them read several books a week on the military exploits of ancient heroes and lecturing them on the virtues of fortitude, endurance, and dialogue over the excesses of violence, but since no sooner were classes over than he had to drive out with them on their bloody expeditions to hunt out salseros in the slums, he felt more and more demoralized. A few weeks after meeting Barbara for the first time he stopped looking at himself in his small campaign mirror in the mornings, perhaps because, like Dorian Gray, he was afraid of looking into his own soul.

One day after making love, Barbara gave him a wise piece of advice. She agreed with him as to the fact that the island could never become independent because it would mean its economic ruin and that therefore they should do everything within their power to prevent the Metropolis from making its decision final. But it was precisely for that reason that the salseros' persecution could be a dangerous thing. "It simply isn't true that there are terrorists infiltrated among them," she said. "In their songs they are exorcising violence by peaceful means, and this is why they are revered by fans. You know as well as I do that our countrymen are a peace-loving people; they may stand by resignedly as their language, their flag, and even their food is taken away from them, but to forbid them salsa is something very different. It's the only way they can vent their frustrations, and if you silence them you may make them explode." Candelario thought Barbara was worried about him and he felt touched. He believed she had been sincere when she had insisted that the party in power was committing a serious political mistake. The party, she had added, might not stay in power forever, and once it had fallen he would be made responsible for the unjust persecution of the musical bands.

A few days after this conversation took place between them, rumors began to go around that a huge salsa concert was being planned, which would be held in spite of the strict government edicts. The rockeros were also expected to attend in full force, and the orchestras of both groups would meet in a musical duel that was expected to last through the night. Musicians were expected from all over the island; the idea was to have so many people participate in the celebration that no prisoners could be taken, and freedom of musical choice would persevere. The concert was to be held in the Condado Lagoon's wide, royal-palmed promenade, next to the new glass-and-steel condominiums that rose on the water's edge.

A few days before the concert Candelario received a second official phone call that made his nerves stand on end. "The time has come for you to show us the effectiveness of the modern war maneuvers you were taught at the military academy," the same cold, hoarse voice said to him. "We have been confidentially informed that the salseros plan to be armed at the concert and that they will attack the rockeros at the first opportunity. Do you understand what I'm telling you, Candelario? It's absolutely imperative that the Missionaries arm the rockeros and that they be the first to attack, so as to wipe out the opposing faction."

Candelario had to make an effort to keep his voice even. "Yes, sir," he answered curtly. "I understand perfectly."

That night he mentioned the telephone call to Barbara. "You must let the concert take place," she told him. "There will be thousands of people there, and if there's going to be violence, no one will be able to control it. The Missionaries will be outnumbered from the start, and you will be made responsible for their fate. But, on the other hand, if the concert takes place normally, nothing may happen." Candelario thought about it for a while and finally decided to listen to her advice. It would be the first time in his life that he would disobey an order, but he felt that persecuting the salseros had been morally wrong from the start.

"I'll do as you say," he told her. "That way no one will be able to say in the future our countrymen let what they call music be taken away from them."

The night before the concert Candelario told Pedro of his decision to disobey orders, feeling sure that he would approve of it. "Let's shake hands and forget what happened between us. Tomorrow we'll enjoy the concert together, and see what the future brings." Pedro had been standing next to the Missionaries' firing range, supervising their target practice and rehearsing the military maneuvers that would take place the next day. Limping slowly, he drew near to his friend and asked him to repeat the order. He was afraid he hadn't heard right, and as he put his Colt .45 back in its holster he looked him straight in the eye.

"I don't know if you've realized the seriousness of your decision, Captain. I advise you to think it over," he said.

Candelario found Pedro's solemnity an exaggeration and he laughed to put him at his ease. "I ordered you to let the salseros sing and dance all they want to tomorrow night. There's going to be so many people there that, if violence should break out, party officials will never know who started it. But on the other hand, if they come only to enjoy themselves, the concert will have been a success."

Pedro looked at him in disbelief. "She talked you into it, didn't she?" he asked. "The redhead from Susana's. She's got you by the balls; I know the symptoms. I'm warning you: if you're going to let the salseros play their music tomorrow night you might as well join them. I've put the men on her track and they're sure she's a salsera. She was born in the slums like I was."

Candelario turned furiously toward him. He took off his jacket and, forgetting where he was, challenged Pedro to a fistfight in front of the Missionaries' firing line, so that several men had to hold him back. "Barbara has absolutely nothing to do with this," he yelled, "and if you call her a salsera once again I'll pound your face into a pulp." And to prove that his decision was final, he ordered the Missionaries to leave their guns in the barracks the following night and to attend the concert unarmed.

When the crowds began to pour into the Condado Lagoon's promenade a few hours before the concert, however, everything had been arranged differently. Recent events had made the Missionaries lose all confidence in Candelario, and they had secretly put themselves under Pedro's orders. After having armed the rockeros as effectively as possible, the Missionaries were to make it a point of locating the salseros in the crowd. They had posted themselves on both sides of the palmed footpaths of Water Bridge or under the street vendors' gaily colored umbrellas, where they downed cod fritters, almojábanas, and blood sausages with cold beer or coconut water. Hiding their firearms in holsters under their armpits or wedged under their belts, they smelled the wind right and left, excited by the nearness of their prey.

Candelario, for his part, strolled nonchalantly amid the dancing couples, greeting everyone and smiling openly under his patent-leather cap. He wasn't at all concerned about his safety; he wanted everybody to know that the rock and salsa festival had been accomplished thanks to his efforts, and that he shared the feeling of national pride that the salsa musicians were putting through in their songs. A sea of flaming Afros and disheveled manes stirred furiously around him as the crowd danced simultaneously to the rhythms of both orchestras, placed at opposing ends of the promenade. After a while he began to look for Pedro and Barbara, because he had lost sight of both of them; they seemed to have been swallowed up by the hundreds of bodies heaving and twisting around him. He was getting tired of all the ass-rolling and fist-shaking, and he walked across the expanse of pavement toward Water Bridge, where there were only a few people about. He gave a deep sigh as he leaned his elbows on the bridge's balustrade, thankful for the sound of the waves breaking softly in the darkness below him. At that moment he heard a familiar voice at his elbow.

"Well, Captain, have you finally made up your mind which music you like best, salsa or rock?"

He turned around feeling relieved that she had found him, but was surprised to see that she was not alone. A group of men holding ice picks stood beside her, among whom were Pedro, his uncle Monchín, and his three cousins. They were pushing a wheelchair before them in which rode the most impressive sight Candelario had ever seen, a legless and armless old man wearing a red T-shirt on which someone had pinned several rows of medals for heroic deeds in Vietnam.

"He hasn't answered my question," Barbara added, laughing, turning to look at Pedro and embracing him by the waist. "I guess now we'll never know."

Candelario had finally realized what was happening to him. He looked at them silently and almost without reproach. "I'm truly sorry, comrade," Pedro said to him in a low voice, "but you never seem to be able to make up your mind. At least now you have the satisfaction of knowing that your countrymen weren't as timid as they appeared to be."

He saw several Missionaries nearby so that he could still have saved himself by crying out for help, but he kept silent. He pinpointed the glint of the ice pick in Pedro's hand, so as to know from which side to expect the first blow, and then

turned his back on Barbara and him with so much con-
tempt that one could have thought he was humbled. For the
first time in many months he felt like a soldier, his soul once
more cast in steel.

"Which do I like?" he said, looking out defiantly toward
the sea. "Neither salsa nor rock. I prefer classical music."